"Carter!" Vanessa ~~screamed~~ his name.

An eerie sound reached her ears from outside the kitchen window. Glancing up, she saw a man, his face covered, staring in at her. She screamed, terror pinging around inside, every nerve end flaring to life.

The man laughed again, a chillingly pleasant laugh. "Goodbye, Vanessa."

All doubt that the killer knew who she was and had targeted her evaporated. He sank out of sight.

A cold sweat broke out on her brow, certainty forming in her soul. The back-door entrance was blocked by the flames. Why couldn't she exit through the front door?

Leaving Carter where he was, she sprinted through the living room to the front door. She reached for the doorknob. Her hand closed on nothing. The doorknob was gone. She tried pushing her fingers through the holes to pry the door open. Nothing.

Somehow, he'd sealed the front door closed.

They were trapped inside a burning house.

Dana R. Lynn grew up in Illinois. She met her husband at a wedding and told her parents she'd met the man she was going to marry. Nineteen months later, they were married. Today, they live in rural Pennsylvania with their three children and a variety of animals. In addition to writing, she works as a teacher for the deaf and hard of hearing, and is active in her church.

Books by Dana R. Lynn

Love Inspired Suspense

Amish Country Danger

Amish Midwife Witness

Amish Country Justice

Plain Refuge
Deadly Amish Reunion
Amish Country Threats
Covert Amish Investigation
Amish Christmas Escape
Amish Cradle Conspiracy
Her Secret Amish Past
Crime Scene Witness
Hidden Amish Target
Hunted at Christmas
Amish Witness to Murder
Protecting the Amish Child
Hunting the Amish Witness

Visit the Author Profile page at LoveInspired.com for more titles.

AMISH MIDWIFE WITNESS

DANA R. LYNN

LOVE INSPIRED SUSPENSE
INSPIRATIONAL ROMANCE

If you purchased this book without a cover you should be aware that this book is stolen property. It was reported as "unsold and destroyed" to the publisher, and neither the author nor the publisher has received any payment for this "stripped book."

LOVE INSPIRED® SUSPENSE
INSPIRATIONAL ROMANCE

ISBN-13: 978-1-335-95741-2

Amish Midwife Witness

Copyright © 2025 by Dana Roae

All rights reserved. No part of this book may be used or reproduced in any manner whatsoever without written permission.

Without limiting the author's and publisher's exclusive rights, any unauthorized use of this publication to train generative artificial intelligence (AI) technologies is expressly prohibited.

This is a work of fiction. Names, characters, places and incidents are either the product of the author's imagination or are used fictitiously. Any resemblance to actual persons, living or dead, businesses, companies, events or locales is entirely coincidental.

For questions and comments about the quality of this book, please contact us at CustomerService@Harlequin.com.

® is a trademark of Harlequin Enterprises ULC.

Love Inspired
22 Adelaide St. West, 41st Floor
Toronto, Ontario M5H 4E3, Canada
www.LoveInspired.com

Printed in Lithuania

For God hath not given us the spirit of fear;
but of power, and of love, and of a sound mind.
—*2 Timothy* 1:7

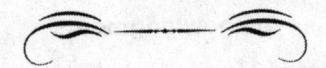

This book is dedicated to the memory of Linda Waldorf.
We'll miss your contagious laugh
and independent spirit.

Acknowledgments

First, thanks to my family for their love, support and willingness to eat mac 'n' cheese during deadline week.

I'd like to thank my agent Tamela Hancock Murray and my editor Tina James for the chance to write this story. I love working with you.

I'm very grateful for my writer friends
who encourage and support me during each book.
Thank you Suspense Squad ladies (Sami Abrams,
Darlene L. Turner, Virginia Vaughan, Patty Boyte,
Shannon Redmon, Loretta Eidson and Hope Welborn).
Thanks also to Belle Calhoune, Lee Tobin McClain,
Jo McNally, Rhonda Starnes, Cate Nolan,
Patricia Johns, Laurel Blount, Mary Alford,
Lisa Jordan, Christy Miller, Katy Lee and Lisa Phillips.
I'm blessed with your friendship!

Thanks to Amy and Dee, my BFFs.
I thank God daily for you!

ONE

Vanessa Hall stalked through the clinic, her nonskid running shoes making virtually no sound, even as she stomped down the hall. Mandy Tennant, her medical assistant, had disappeared...again. Not even the festive decorations or the soft strains of Christmas music put a dent in her anger and frustration.

If I find out she's skipped out to call her boyfriend again, I'll report her.

It wouldn't be so bad if it wasn't only ten days before Christmas. Or if it didn't happen all the time.

She stopped a nurse coming out of one of the small examination rooms. "Amy, have you seen Mandy?"

Amy tilted her head. "Hmm. Maybe five minutes ago? She was headed to the supply closet, I think."

Vanessa thanked her and made her way down the hallway, where all the patient examination rooms were located, and turned to the left, toward the staff-only area.

Ahead, she heard Mandy's voice, pitched low, coming from inside Sterling Ridge Medical Clinic's only supply room. A male voice responded, although Vanessa couldn't make out the words.

She was on the phone. *I knew it! If she's not put on an improvement plan or fired, I'll be shocked.*

It was a shame. She'd really liked the young woman when they'd hired her, but they couldn't allow this kind of dereliction of duty to continue. The reputation of the clinic would suffer. Not to mention the risk to the patients. Determined, Vanessa strode to the door, intending to shove it open to confront the medical assistant. Mandy's words made her freeze in her tracks.

"I know I'm not supposed to call you at this number. I'm sorry. But listen, this is important. I just heard that Opal Bontrager is on her way in. She's having some kind of emergency and is probably in labor. You have to come now, if you want her baby. If she delivers here, you might not have another chance to snatch it."

Vanessa's jaw dropped. She couldn't have heard that right. Mandy might be irresponsible, but engaged in something so evil? She couldn't believe it.

"This isn't convenient," a muffled voice said. Mandy must have her phone's speaker on, although it was low. For once, Vanessa was thankful for the girl's lack of common courtesy when talking on the phone. She always used the speaker because she didn't like holding a phone to her ear. The unknown speaker continued, his voice growing louder, angrier. "The buyer isn't expecting a baby for several weeks. We'd have to take the mother before she delivered. Taking a mother and child from a clinic will be difficult. Security is heavy."

"I know you don't usually take the mothers. But if she's ready to deliver, this is the only shot you'll get. Unless you don't need this baby anymore."

There was a pause. Then a heavy sigh.

"No, we need this one. Our next target won't be born for another three months."

"Uh-huh. I figured. Just remember I haven't been paid yet." The cold words were mixed with a sneering tone.

White-hot fury flashed through Vanessa. She slapped her open palm against the partially open door. It slammed open so hard the handle banged against the counter. The door bounced back, but Vanessa pushed it in and stepped inside the small room. Mandy spun around, her face paling. She backed away from Vanessa, but due to the multiple shelves filled with supplies, she had barely any space to retreat.

"Vanessa—"

Vanessa held up a hand, halting the assistant.

"You're done here," Vanessa snarled. "I heard the conversation. I'm calling the police."

"I can explain!"

"Explain it to the police. You'll be going to jail." She nodded at the phone in the other woman's hand. "Who are you talking to? He sounds familiar. If I figure out who he is, he's going to jail with you."

The sound of a dial tone was the only response. Obviously, the kidnapper had hung up. Mandy pressed her lips together, her whole body shaking. Vanessa scowled at her with zero sympathy. Mandy's monstrous actions and plans deserved no pity.

To assist in a kidnapping was unforgivable. And what did they plan on doing with Opal once they stole her baby? Ice filled her veins. Surely, Mandy wouldn't willingly be complicit with murder. Were they running an illegal adoption business? Human trafficking? What motive could she possibly have? Pain mingled with her outrage. Vanessa knew she would never have children of her own. She'd once planned on having a large family, like the one she'd grown up in. But after a night she could never quite remember, when her boyfriend had betrayed her so heinously, then abandoned her, leaving her pregnant and hurting, she'd lost her faith in men.

She'd miscarried a few weeks later, destroying her faith in a good and loving God.

Being the victim of date rape had devastated her. If she was honest with herself, it continued to haunt her and affected her life daily. She still had nightmares about it.

Her family never knew why she'd changed her degree from veterinary medicine and opted to become a certified nurse midwife instead. All her parents knew was that their straight-A student had let her grades slip. She allowed them to believe that she had gone through a normal period of becoming too focused on the social aspects of college life. She would never tell them that she'd survived the horror by directing her fury and her despair into helping other women bring their babies into the world.

She glared at Mandy, deliberately stepping into her personal space until the younger woman cringed back against the shelves. Vanessa clenched her fists. Knowing Mandy was willing to put both Opal and her child in danger, not to mention the harm she'd do to their family, infuriated her.

Vanessa shoved her anger down inside. She'd deal with it later. Right now, she needed to get this woman off their premises and make sure Opal Bontrager, a pregnant Amish woman and mother of three, arrived safely and was protected from the predator out to injure her.

She peered out into the hall. Dr. Findley, the anesthesiologist who had come in that morning for an outpatient procedure, rounded the hallway and strode in their direction. He stopped, confused, when she stepped into his path.

"Nurse?" he asked in his soft, modulated voice. "Did you need something?"

"Doctor, can you please give me your phone? I need to call nine-one-one. I'd do it, but my phone is in my bag."

George Findley's dark eyebrows climbed his high forehead, nearly reaching his receding hairline. "What? You're already in a medical facility."

"No time to go into detail. We have a very pregnant woman on the way in. She's in danger and needs police protection. I'll explain later."

Dr. Findley didn't hesitate. He grabbed his device from the pocket in his white coat and handed it over to Vanessa. She dialed.

"Nine-one-one. What's the nature of your emergency?"

"This is Nurse Vanessa Hall, certified nurse midwife, at Sterling Ridge Medical Clinic. I have a pregnant woman on the way in, possibly going into early labor, who is in danger. I just overheard a phone conversation. Someone is planning on abducting her and stealing her baby."

The doctor's mouth dropped open. His eyes shifted behind her to stare at the trembling medical assistant. He turned around and headed back up the hall, disappearing around the corner. A few moments later, he reappeared with the security guard from the waiting room. When the guard arrived at the supply room, the doctor quietly told him to keep watch over Mandy until the police arrived to take her into custody.

After talking with the dispatcher, Vanessa hurried to the lobby and stood beside the Christmas tree that Shannon, the receptionist, had set up two days ago. From her position, she could keep an eye on the entrance. Unfortunately, Opal wouldn't arrive in an ambulance, which would have provided her with more security. Instead, the woman's husband had no doubt called one of the local civilians near the Amish community that were often hired to drive the Amish to their appointments, or places too far to go by horse and buggy. Sterling Ridge, a small town in northwestern Pennsylvania, was in a mostly rural area and had an extensive Amish and Mennonite population.

It was after four by the time she heard an engine purring outside. A blue cruiser with white letters on the side turned into the parking lot. Sterling Ridge Police Department. Relief poured through her. "Finally."

"Give them some grace," Shannon said, pushing her glasses up her nose. "You know it's a small department."

Vanessa rolled her shoulders to release the tension building. "True. And I've heard a few accidents on the monitor. So they're pretty busy."

Opal would be safe now that law enforcement had arrived. Vanessa ignored the fluffy white snow drifting down and rushed outside. Snow hit the bare skin on her face, neck and hands, but she ignored the cold.

The cruiser lights remained on, splashing red and blue on the sand-colored brick walls and the shimmery snowdrifts. The doors opened and two officers stepped from the vehicle. One of them approached her. The other remained at the carport.

She understood a second later when Opal's driver pulled his vehicle under the carport. Immediately, two nurses with a wheeled stretcher and Dr. Spencer, the head doctor at the clinic, arrived. The other police officer strode to the group, his gaze scanning the parking lot for any activity. He followed the team handling Opal and her husband into the center.

"You stay and talk with the cop," Dr. Spencer told her. "Chelsea has been advised and can handle this case until you arrive."

Vanessa nodded. Chelsea Russell was the other CNM at the small clinic. Vanessa didn't like passing off her cases to others, but this was an extreme circumstance. She turned to face the officer. He stood a good three inches taller than her own five foot eight inches.

"Thanks for coming, Officer—"

"Lieutenant Carter Flint, nurse. Can you tell me what happened?" Although his words seemed impersonal, compassion gleamed from his dark blue eyes.

Vanessa repeated the conversation she'd overheard.

"Did you hear a name, anything that would help us identify who she was talking to?"

She shook her head. "Nothing. I haven't touched her phone. Didn't think that would be the smart thing to do. She's with Security now. Harold, the security guard, won't let her use her phone."

They walked through the doors separating the waiting room from the patient-examination rooms. Surgery was in the other wing of the structure. They walked past the row of patient rooms and the nurses' station to the supply room. Inside, Mandy was sitting on a chair in the middle of the room, arms crossed over her chest, pale but defiant. Harold nodded at the lieutenant.

"I'll return to my duties now that you've arrived to take charge."

Some of the bravado fled Mandy's face when Lieutenant Flint approached her. "Please stand, miss."

Vanessa watched, impressed by his calm demeanor while he cuffed the young assistant and read Mandy her rights. Vanessa followed him back through the clinic in case he thought of any other questions. And because she needed to see for herself that Mandy was put in the cruiser and taken to face the consequences of her actions.

She shuddered, thinking of Opal and Mandy's plans for her. Anger burned in her chest. While she and Mandy weren't friends, she'd trusted her.

Once again, she'd been betrayed.

The sliding doors opened with a soft hiss. Lieutenant Flint

glanced around for a few seconds before leading his prisoner toward the cruiser. Vanessa followed him out the door and watched.

He kept one hand on Mandy when he arrived at the cruiser. Reaching around her, he grabbed the door handle.

Crack!

A gunshot broke the silence. Mandy hit the ground, a bullet hole in the middle of her forehead.

Vanessa screamed and stepped back. The doors opened again an instant before a second gunshot rang out, shattering the clinic door directly behind her. Lieutenant Flint flung himself toward her, pushing her through the open door.

She couldn't remove her gaze from the vacant stare of the young woman lying dead on the pavement. Bile rose in her throat. She bit her fist to keep from screaming again. How did the shooter know Mandy had been arrested?

One thought seared into her brain. Whomever Mandy had been working with had gone to extreme lengths to ensure his partner couldn't identify him.

Carter shoved the attractive red-haired nurse away from the door. "Keep low. Get behind the reception desk."

She nodded and scurried off, giving the body outside one last horrified glance.

She passed the front desk and made a shooing motion at the receptionist, "Shannon, get away from the desk. You're too out in the open. Get down and stay out of sight."

His eyebrows rose. She had backbone. And common sense. That was good to know. Too many people would have frozen or completely broken down at the sight of someone gunned down before their eyes. He watched her hurrying the other clinic personnel out of the area. Her voice wobbled once. Then she cleared her throat, and the next time she spoke, steel threaded through her words.

There were no other patients in the waiting room. They'd already been moved to the back of the clinic. Brett must have done that.

He grabbed his phone and called Dispatch. When he heard the familiar voice on the line, he spoke quickly. "Lori, this is Carter Flint. I need more backup. We have a shooter at large. I also need the coroner. We have a civilian down."

It wasn't until he felt his jaw aching that he realized he'd clenched his teeth. One woman was dead. He should have been more thorough checking his surroundings. She had been an accessory to an attempted kidnapping, maybe more than one, but she didn't deserve to die that way, cut down sniper-style. She couldn't have been more than twenty-two or twenty-three. Just a kid, really.

That's what bothered him. Another young life snuffed out before they'd had the chance to change their ways.

He shook his head. The young medical assistant's death couldn't be undone, the same way his teenage sister's death by suicide after months of intense cyberbullying couldn't be wished away. If only she'd spoken up, instead of hiding what had happened.

According to his mother, he should have done better to protect his baby sister. If he'd paid more attention to her while his mom worked two jobs to keep a roof over their heads, her death wouldn't have happened. Even becoming a cop to help others hadn't lessened her bitterness toward him.

Nor had moving her into his house after she'd been diagnosed with dementia. If anything, she took advantage of their proximity to pour out her hostility in little digs and cuts daily.

Once Nancy Flint got a thought into her head, nothing could convince her to change her mind.

If this came from the woman who had once claimed to love him forever, then no relationship, no woman, could be trusted to keep her promises. He'd care for his mom, but he'd live out his life single.

But with God's help, someday, he vowed, someday, he'd redeem himself in his mother's eyes.

He forced his thoughts away from his mother and his sister, Gretta, and forced himself to focus on the case at hand. They had a dead woman, a pregnant Amish woman in danger and a shooter at large. He crouched down near the large picture window and peered out into the rapidly dimming light.

Even while he watched, streetlamps burst to life, flooding the parking lot and carport with light. That would make it more difficult for a shooter to take them by surprise. They still needed to proceed with caution, though. The area outside the lights' reach remained in shadow.

His phone rang. It was his partner, Lieutenant Brett Talbot. "Yeah, Brett. What have you got?"

"The patient was just loaded onto a helicopter. They're flying her to Erie. She's going into early labor. I'm going to go along and make sure she has security. The doctor thinks both she and her baby will need to stay there for a couple of days."

"Got it. I called in for backup. I'll process the scene and search for the shooter."

At least with the pregnant woman out of reach, that should lower the danger for everyone else in the clinic.

If this turned out to be an isolated incident, he'd relax. But unfortunately, several babies had been abducted in the past few months. It was hard to pin down where the kidnapper would strike next. He never seemed to hit the same area twice. The first two kidnappings had happened in rural hospitals and clinics. The little ID bracelets had been cut off in the middle of the night and the children whisked away. The second baby had been found before the abductor, a young janitor who worked in the hospital, could abscond with her. Since then, the security in the hospitals in the surrounding counties tightened.

For a while, it seemed the abductions had slowed, while some hoped they'd ended altogether. Carter disagreed. He thought those heading up the operation were regrouping and maybe moving to a new location.

Sadly, he had been proven correct.

A month after the first kidnappings, a Mennonite couple reported a newborn missing. The little girl had disappeared during the night while her family slept. They found evidence that the parents had been drugged. How remained a mystery.

Since then, two more babies had been taken, both from Amish families. The cruel ruthlessness chilled him to his very soul. In rural Pennsylvania, most Amish and Mennonite women gave birth in their homes with the assistance of midwives instead of doctors. Sometimes the midwives were Amish women, although some were from local medical clinics. The red-haired beauty who had called 911 came to mind.

How were the kidnappers finding their targets? In the first two cases, all the prenatal care had occurred at either the mother's ob-gyn or family doctor office. He'd need to get a search warrant for the Sterling Ridge medical records to see if there were any connections between the last few cases. It was possible the women came to the clinics for prenatal care and Mandy had sold the information.

A quiet sob broke into his thoughts. He poked his head through the reception window. The young receptionist—Shannon?—sat on a round stool, her face buried in her hands, shoulders heaving.

"Miss?" He stopped himself from asking if she were all

right. Of course she wasn't. Anyone would be traumatized by these events.

She lifted her head. "I'm sorry. Do you need something?"

"I'm sorry for your loss. How well did you know Mandy?"

She hiccupped then shrugged. "Not well. I've only been here a few weeks."

"I understand. But have you noticed anything off about her behavior lately?"

She shook her head. "No. But I know she complained about money a lot."

He asked a few more questions about the deceased. Shannon couldn't tell him much beyond her name and age.

A nurse entered the room and handed Shannon a steaming mug. Mint scented the air. Herbal tea, probably. He thanked her and continued processing the scene.

Carter left the building when he saw two more cruisers enter the parking lot. He greeted his colleagues. Sergeant Stella Thompson and Officer Michaela Witt began setting up the crime-scene tape and taking photos. Officer Joseph Maillard walked the perimeter and Lieutenant Ryan Douglass peeled away from his colleagues to go inside and complete the interviews with the staff and patients.

The coroner pulled in less than five minutes later. Carter waited for Deanna Snow to exit her vehicle. He liked Deanna, had voted for her in the last election, but still, it saddened him whenever he saw her enter a crime scene.

Her job had to take a toll on a person mentally.

"Carter." She bobbed her head at him in greeting.

"Afternoon, Deanna. Sorry to bring you out this late in the day."

She shrugged. "My job is a twenty-four-seven kind of job. What do you have for me?"

He led her to the body and recited the information he'd

gathered from Nurse Hall and Shannon. "This is Mandy Tennant, age twenty-three. She was shot once in the head while being escorted in police custody at around four thirty this afternoon."

Deana glanced at her watch. "Almost six now."

While she examined the corpse, Carter took out his phone to check in with Brett and Ryan. Brett responded almost immediately that his patient had arrived at the hospital in Erie and had been taken in for an emergency C-section. No word yet on either the mother or the infant. Ryan texted ten minutes later to tell him the last of the three patients on the premises had been released out the back entrance, walked to her car and sent home.

He shoved his phone back into his jacket pocket, glad that there were fewer civilians hanging around. He waited until Deanna had completed her work with Mandy and gave him the thumbs-up before returning to the warmth of the medical center. Although, with the door blown out, a biting wind had invaded the structure.

They'd have to do something about that before they could service patients.

His eyes met the steady gaze of the pretty redheaded nurse. Her pallor belied her serene expression. He made his way over to her. "Nurse Hall—"

"Vanessa."

He nodded. "Vanessa. How are you holding up?"

She quirked an eyebrow. "I'm fine. Shaken. Shocked. Appalled that my coworker had been involved in something shady, but sad about her death."

Wow. Most people would say "fine" and leave it at that. Nurse Hall—Vanessa—intrigued him. There was something precise about the way she spoke.

"How did he know?"

Carter understood immediately what she was referring to. "I can only think of one way. Whoever she'd been talking to knew she'd been found out. The next obvious step would be arrest. But for him to get here that fast, he had to be stationed close by."

She nodded. "Maybe not. It took you almost thirty minutes to arrive."

He knew she hadn't meant her comment to sound critical, but he winced. It still set his teeth on edge, the time it took to respond to calls. But in rural Pennsylvania, they didn't have the manpower necessary to answer calls as quickly as they had in the city. Plus, the area was spread out and sometimes weather conditions interfered, such as the blowing snow they had outside right now.

"I can give you an escort home—" he began.

"That's unnecessary." She made a short, chopping motion, cutting off his words. She sounded almost abrupt, but he could tell she was still upset, so he didn't let it annoy him. Much.

"It would be safer for you. You did interrupt Mandy's call."

"I did. But she refused to tell me who she was talking to. And the shooter only shot her, not me."

"The clinic door was shattered by a second gunshot. You were standing right in front of it. I can't rule out that you were the intended victim."

She shivered. Good. Sometimes a healthy dose of fear saved lives.

"I'll be careful."

That wasn't what he wanted. "Vanessa."

She shook her head. "Please. Just ask what you need to know."

He frowned. He didn't like her choice, but it was her choice. "Please reconsider. I think you're making a mistake."

She crossed her arms and waited.

He focused on getting her statement. "Did she say anything to you while she was on the phone?"

She shrugged. "My name. That was it."

"Vanessa isn't a common name. I think you should have some sort of escort, at least tonight, to be on the safe side."

"I think it would be a waste of valuable resources. I'll be fine."

Fine. He hated that word. It was used far too often and usually meant the exact opposite. But he couldn't change her mind, nor could he force someone to accept police protection. "At least allow me to walk you out to your vehicle."

She nodded and heaved an overlarge purse onto her shoulder. He walked silently beside her out to a dark blue Jeep and checked her back seat and under the vehicle before stepping back to give her room to enter. She thanked him and started her engine. When she pulled forward, he remained standing, watching until her car disappeared down the street.

He had a bad feeling about this.

Vanessa rested her aching back against the heated seat and clenched her fists on the steering wheel. Finally, after the gruesome, horrifying afternoon, she was alone. She couldn't hold back the hot tears that welled up and poured down her cheeks. She could barely see. Hitting her blinker, she pulled off the road and allowed the avalanche of emotions to take over. When she calmed, five minutes had passed.

"Stop it, Nessa. You are too old to be so out of control. Get it together."

Her self-talk failed. Another wobbly sob burst out, but she refused to give in and allow another tear to escape. She'd survived, and Opal and her baby would be safe.

She hoped.

Mandy was dead. She winced as the memory of the pretty young assistant's blank eyes hit her. Yes, she'd done something horrible, and Vanessa had been furious with her. But she'd never wanted this outcome.

She didn't know Mandy that well. Did she live with her parents? Have brothers or sisters?

Or had she been alone in the world? Vanessa regretted not taking the time to get to know her better. If she had, maybe she'd have known something was wrong.

But Vanessa didn't invest too much time in getting to know her colleagues below the surface. There weren't many people she trusted, and she planned to keep it that way. But still, she couldn't help but wonder if she could have stopped this before it ended with a woman dead.

She shuddered, knowing Mandy's murderer had eluded capture. Would he still go after Opal? At least the police were aware of the danger. Her one fear was that the Amish family would refuse any offer of help or protection for the mother or child.

She bit her lip. Not that she could judge. She'd refused that handsome police lieutenant's offer of an escort.

An odd desire to say a prayer for the woman came to mind, but she brushed it aside. She'd managed to live without God in her life for seven years. It wasn't like He helped her when she needed Him most. If He really cared, someone would have seen Nolan spike her drink. Her whole life would have been different.

Putting on her blinker again, she maneuvered back onto the road. Main Street lasted for approximately four blocks before connecting with a few suburban-type roads. She lived in a small house outside the town of Sterling Ridge. The farther she drove, the more rural the landscape became. She smiled as the word *rural* went through her mind. She had a clear view of her neighbor's cows out her living-room window.

If that wasn't rural, she didn't know what was.

A deer bolted in front of her. She stomped on her brakes to avoid the animal. And caught her breath at the car coming at her from behind. They must not have seen her brake lights. If she didn't move, they'd hit her.

Accelerating, she glanced in her mirror again. Then frowned. The car still hadn't slowed. In fact, it continued to close on her. What was going on?

She pressed the gas to go faster. She'd be turning off in less than a mile.

The car edged closer.

That's when she saw the short barrel of a handgun aimed at her. Her breath hitched in her throat and the blood pounded in her ears.

Lieutenant Flint had been right. Despite Mandy's death, she was in danger. And the killer was hot on her tail, planning on making her his next victim.

TWO

Vanessa screamed and swerved her Jeep away from the car. Her tires ground against rumble strips on the shoulder, and she nearly lost control as her passenger side dropped down several inches. She gripped the wheel and yanked her Jeep back onto the road, nearly swiping against the shooter's car moving up next to hers. In her periphery, a black gun muzzle waggled.

He was really going to shoot her!

A gunshot rang out. The bullet smashed into her door. Never had she been so glad to have a vehicle with higher seats. If she'd still had her smaller car, her window would have been level with the shooter's, and she'd probably be dead right now.

The oppressive darkness around them obscured the driver's face. All she could see of his lower face seemed to be covered with some kind of mask or handkerchief. She couldn't be sure which. The rest of his facial features were hidden.

There was no descriptive information to give the police if she made it out of this situation alive.

She pushed the gas pedal. Her Jeep surged forward, past the car. She held the steering wheel in a white-knuckled grip. She should call 911. But to do that, she'd have to release the wheel. Sweat trickled down the side of her face.

She took her right hand off the wheel and jabbed the Bluetooth call button. When it beeped, she yelled, "Dial!"

The computerized voice responded, "What number?"

"Nine-one-one!"

A quick glance in her rearview mirror showed the car roaring up behind her again. They went around a sharp bend. Lights came from the other direction. A pickup truck with a Christmas tree ratcheted down in its bed, prickly branches overflowing the sides, zoomed past. A popular country music song blasted from the truck's speakers.

That truck was the only thing that saved her from the car coming alongside her before they headed into the narrowest curve of the two-laned road. In less than two miles, the road would widen back up. Nothing would stop her assailant then.

"What's the nature of your emergency?"

"I'm in my Jeep heading north on the Park Avenue extension, just past Braken Trails. There's a car following me. He has a gun. He's already shot at me once and hit my door."

"Ma'am, who am I talking to?"

Vanessa wanted to howl it didn't matter, but she held in her frustration. "Vanessa Hall. I'm a nurse at Sterling Ridge Medical Clinic."

"I'm dispatching police officers to your location. Don't pull over."

Like she'd planned to.

She rounded the last curve. Her high beams swept the snowy landscape ahead. No oncoming traffic blocked the other lane, which stretched out before her, a straight line for as far as she could see.

Her time of grace had ended.

As if she'd conjured him up with her thoughts, the other car shifted into the other lane.

"He's coming up beside me!"

Vanessa pressed the gas pedal again. The needle on the speedometer crept upward. The vehicle shimmied on the icy roads. She dared not go faster. If someone came out of one of the houses or if an impatient driver turned onto the road ahead of her, she wouldn't be able to control her vehicle.

"Ma'am! Stay calm. Help is on the way."

Stay calm? A laugh bubbled up in her throat. Vanessa swallowed it down. The woman was correct. She needed to keep a clear head. Her heart pumped so hard in her chest, she could barely hear the dispatcher over it.

"Is the driver next to you?"

"Nearly." She risked a couple more notches on the speedometer. "I'm traveling at fifty-eight miles per hour."

The road's speed limit was posted at forty-five. Ever since she'd lost her baby in college, Vanessa had been a stickler about following the rules, including traffic rules. She'd learned the hard way that broken rules came back and tormented you.

She glanced to the side. The car had pulled alongside and was keeping pace with her. She saw the gun pointed her way again.

"He's going to shoot me!"

The dispatcher's reply was lost amid the loud blast from the gun. Pain burned across her left shoulder. Had he hit her axillary artery?

Her eyes watered, blurring her view. She blinked rapidly. A tear tumbled down her cheek. She ignored it. Right now, she needed to focus on staying alive. She shook her head, trying to remain alert. The dispatcher yelled over the speakers, "Vanessa! Are you alright? Can you hear me?"

"I can hear you," she finally replied. "He shot me. In the shoulder."

Were her words slurring? When her vehicle slowed, she

realized she'd removed her foot from the gas pedal. She lifted her eyes. The shooter edged into her lane. Oh, no. He was trying to cut her off. She'd be a sitting duck if he managed to block her. His vehicle began to pull into her path.

She slammed her foot down on the gas, and her Jeep jolted forward, the front bumper smacking into his passenger side. Metal screeched against metal. She cringed at the sound, but kept going, fighting to control her vehicle while pain pulsed through her body.

"Ma'am. Talk to me. Are you okay?"

The dispatcher's voice grounded her. "My shoulder hurts. I don't know what the bullet hit." She blinked again. It was getting harder to keep her eyes focused. "He tried to cut me off, but I got past him."

A quick glance in the rearview mirror cut off any hopes that he'd given up.

"He's still coming after me."

In the distance, sirens wailed. Good. The police were on the way.

"I've dispatched an ambulance along with the police. Both should be heading your way. The police are less than two minutes from your position."

"What is taking them so long?" she muttered.

"I'm sorry, ma'am. They're coming as fast as they can."

Vanessa grimaced. She hadn't meant to grumble out loud, but pain was messing with her impulses. Her shoulder throbbed. Her left fist, clenched around the steering wheel, began to go numb. Whether from her grip or because of her wound, she didn't know.

How much longer could she hold out against the evil racing after her?

Her assailant came at her again. He rammed his vehicle

into her. She screamed. The sturdy Jeep shuddered at the attack. She kept it on the road, but it was close.

Dimly, she heard the dispatcher calling her.

"He hit me with his car."

She had no time to say any more. The car's engine revved, and he plunged toward her again, striking her door. Metal crunched. The wheel flew from her grasp. The Jeep hurtled off the road. The passenger side of the car banged against the guardrail on the right side. The Jeep continued its journey. A huge oak tree lay ahead. Vanessa screamed again.

Her scream ended in a gasping cry when her vehicle collided with the tree. Vanessa flew forward. Her head bounced off the frame surrounding the window before the seat belt yanked her back to her seat, probably bruising her ribs. The airbag deployed, forcing her back. The front end of her Jeep folded like tissue paper.

The car that had come after her stopped. For a moment, she thought he'd get out of his car and come to finish her off. Instead, the engine roared and he took off.

A moment later, she saw lights heading her way.

The police. They'd come to save her. Hopefully, she wouldn't perish from her wounds before the ambulance arrived. A buzz filled her ears and spread through her head. Her body grew light. The darkness overtook her.

Carter arrived on the scene, his heart pumping so hard it hurt. He'd known Vanessa Hall was still in danger. Every instinct in him had screamed at him to not let her leave alone. But as a law-enforcement officer, he couldn't force an adult to accept protection.

His mind knew that. His heart, though, accused him that once again he'd failed someone and might have been unintentionally responsible for a young woman's death.

Gretta's bloodless face and staring eyes popped into his mind. Ruthlessly, he shoved the image of his teenage sister away. He had a life to save.

"I'm at the scene of the shooting," he said, radioing in. "I don't see the shooter in the area, but the victim's Jeep is crashed into a tree. I can't see any movement inside the vehicle."

"Sending backup. An ambulance has already been dispatched."

He knew the ambulance might be a while. There had been multiple car accidents and calls that night due to the weather. The small town only had one ambulance service, and it was taxed to its limit.

He prayed he wouldn't need to call the coroner again.

Carter parked his cruiser along the side of the road, then hopped out and grabbed the first-aid kit before cautiously approaching the Jeep. The new snow had created a hazardous surface. Steam hissed from the smashed front end of the car. The radiator must be damaged.

He looked in the driver's window. Vanessa glanced back at him, her eyes unfocused and confused. The deflated airbag hung limply from the center of the steering wheel, obscuring his view of her legs. He tried to open the door. It wouldn't budge.

"Vanessa!" he yelled. "Unlock the door."

It took her a few seconds to register his words. When she hit the button, he pulled on the handle. Still nothing. He aimed his flashlight at the edge of her door, which was bent inward at a strange angle, as if another car had hit it there. It was amazing the window hadn't broken. His stomach dropped. Opening the door manually would be impossible.

Maybe she could crawl to the other side. He made his way around the back of the car. The right side was snug against another large tree, blocking it.

The only way out was through the driver's-side door. He had to get it opened. A glance inside the Jeep showed him another complication. Vanessa's eyes were closed. He banged on the window.

"Vanessa! Open your eyes! Look at me."

There was no response. He saw a bloody spot on her forehead. There was also a widening spot on her left shoulder. Even through her warm winter coat, he saw it. She needed help now. Where was that ambulance?

His phone rang. He recognized Chief Melody Kaiser's ringtone.

"Flint here, Chief."

"Sean is a minute from your position. Status?"

"I need the fire department to bring rescue equipment. I have an unconscious woman bleeding from a bullet wound in her left shoulder. I can't get to her."

Vanessa's eyes fluttered.

The chief began to speak, but Carter interrupted. "Ma'am, she's stirring! Hold on." He banged on the window again. Vanessa turned in his direction, moving in slow motion. Her bleary blue eyes were glazed with pain. He gestured at the window, imitating it opening. "Open the window!"

He had to repeat himself twice before she understood and complied.

Sergeant Sean Craig's vehicle rumbled up and parked behind his. Carter kept his attention focused on the woman. He pulled off his gloves and replaced them with the sterile ones from the first-aid kit. Then he withdrew some sterile gauze pads.

"Carter," she mumbled. "My shoulder hurts. And my head."

"Vanessa, you're bleeding. You were shot. I'm going to apply some pressure to stop the bleeding. It may hurt."

"Do it." She grunted when he put a stack of the pads in

place, then had her lean back against them. Until they got her out of the car, that would have to suffice.

"Hang on, Vanessa. Help is on the way."

"What do you need me to do, Lieutenant?" Sean asked.

"Can you take care of traffic?" Carter said to Sean.

Sean nodded. "I'll handle it. Ambulance should be here anytime now."

While Sean went to take on traffic control, Carter leaned in through the window and did a quick check to ensure that Vanessa had no other injuries. "Do you remember getting shot?"

Her eyes widened. "Yes! Someone was shooting at me! He forced me off the road and rammed the side of my Jeep. I couldn't see his face. Only the gun pointed at me."

She lurched forward, catching herself on the still-buckled seat belt.

"Whoa! Hold on, Vanessa." He placed a gentle hand on her shoulder. "We'll get you checked out and cared for. I'm concerned you'll make the wound bleed more. Once I know you're good, we'll get a description of the shooter and take your statement."

A horn beeped, dragging his attention away from Vanessa's face. The ambulance parked. Sean waved at the two paramedics, Jason and Tyler, and continued directing traffic.

He moved out of the way as the ambulance crew checked her vitals. "Good work on stopping the bleeding."

"Thanks, Jason. I can't get her out." He gestured to mangled door.

"We have one victim with entrapment." Jason said into his radio.

"Help is on the way."

Two minutes later, a fire department vehicle pulled in. They went to work on getting her from the car. Carter hovered as they loaded her onto the ambulance. He ducked his head through the doors before Jason sealed the ambulance. "Vanessa, I'll have your Jeep towed as soon as it can be. The paramedics will take you to Good Samaritan hospital. When I'm done, I'll come out to the hospital to talk with you and take your statement."

She closed her eyes briefly. "I get it. The Jeep is part of a crime scene now."

When Tyler moved in to secure the doors, Carter stepped away, his boots crunching on the snow. A single flake fluttered down, dusting his cheek and melting upon contact.

Glancing up, he frowned. The snowflakes began to fall in a soft, steady pattern. He dropped his eyes to the weather app on his phone. A new storm system was heading their way. The next two days promised between eight and twelve more inches of snow.

He loved rural northwestern Pennsylvania. He really did. But the weather could be a little intense.

By the time the crime-scene unit arrived, his cruiser lay under a light blanket of white, fluffy flakes. He called his chief and updated her on the situation. When he told her about the conversation Vanessa had overheard, the chief didn't respond for a full thirty seconds.

"Buying and selling babies. That's a new level of nastiness."

"Yes, ma'am. She's on her way to Good Sam. I'm going there in a few minutes. I need to get a full statement," he told his superior officer. "Chief, my gut says this guy, whoever he is, isn't finished. Vanessa heard an incriminating conversation and then saw him up close in his car. He's already tried to take her out once and will probably try again."

"I agree it doesn't look good. We'll have to put some security measures in place. Hopefully, they'll keep her overnight at the hospital. That will give us some time to strategize."

Carter hung up. One of the CSU members called out to him. "We have a bullet. I'll get it processed for you, but don't expect to hear anything until next week."

Carter bit back a huff of irritation. It wouldn't help. The system was notoriously slow. He would have to be patient.

And vigilant. Whoever tried to kill Vanessa remained at large. He needed to catch him before he came back to finish the job.

THREE

Vanessa opened her eyes and shifted on the narrow hospital bed in her room in the post anesthesia care unit, groaning. Finding a comfortable position proved impossible. Her shoulder ached.

The memory of a gun pointed in her direction surged into her brain and Vanessa shot upward into a sitting position, ignoring the agony jolting through her body. Someone had killed Mandy and had tried to exterminate her as well.

"Knock, knock." A cheerful nurse pushed open the door and stuck her head inside, disrupting her thoughts. "I'm glad you're awake."

"Yeah. My shoulder hurts." Vanessa forced down the panic.

The nurse nodded, her brown ponytail bobbing with the motion of her head. She pushed the door open more and came completely into the room. An ID that indicated her name was Sabrina hung from a lanyard around her neck. "I'd imagine so. After all, you were shot. The doctor had to put in nine stitches. It will leave a wicked scar."

"Are you new?" Vanessa winced. She hadn't meant to blurt that out. It probably sounded rude. "Sorry. I work at the clinic. I thought I knew all the nurses and doctors in the area, both there at here at the hospital."

"No worries." Sabrina grinned. "I just started here last week."

Although, there probably weren't that many such injuries in Sterling Ridge. They were a very rural community. The largest city nearby was Meadville, and that was almost an hour's drive away.

Sighing, she settled back against the nearly flat hospital grade pillow. She was inside Good Samaritan Hospital. For the moment, she was safe.

"What time is it?"

"A little after nine thirty." Sabrina smiled again. "I'm off to the next patient. Use the call button if you need anything."

The perky nurse left the room, closing the door quietly behind her.

Outside Vanessa's window, it was dark. Part of her yearned to return home. She might be a nurse, but she didn't relish the idea of spending the night in the hospital. On the other hand, the idea of being in her house, alone, knowing someone wanted her dead, tormented her. Enough that she might have given in and called one of her siblings to stay with her, if they weren't all busy.

Vanessa had trouble accepting that level of care. Part of it was she liked her independence too much. *And you're not as worthy as they think you are*, a voice whispered in her soul.

She knew that. She'd tried to make up for her mistakes for nearly seven years, but still, what she'd done, what she'd allowed to happen, continued to haunt her. It also made trusting strangers, particularly men, difficult. She'd already proven her inability to discern good husband material from a player.

Someone rapped three times on the door.

"Come in." She tried to straighten in the bed, wincing when her stitches pulled. She gave up and remained reclined on the bed. She despised the vulnerability rippling through her. Vanessa always met challenges from a position of strength.

The door opened and Lieutenant Flint poked his head around. His dark blond hair was a little longer than regulation, and the slight scruff on his jaw wasn't the norm for officers. What really got to her were his eyes. They were halfway between gray and blue, reminding her of a stormy sky. Nothing like the piercing blue orbs she and all her siblings had in common.

"Hey! You're awake!" He sent a contagious smile her way. "How are you feeling?"

"Like I've been run over by a train." She forced a smile to her lips.

"I can imagine." He grabbed the chair near the bed and dragged it into position beside her, then settled himself in as if they were having a casual conversation. "I was here a couple of hours ago, but you were out like a light. Are you feeling up to answering some questions?"

"Oh, yeah. But can you find out if I can go home soon?"

"Already did. The doctors said that if you have someone to stay with you, they'll let you go tonight."

That put her in a situation. "Ugh. I'll be fine by myself. Honest. I'm a nurse. I know what to look for."

The smile slid off his face. "There's no one you can call?"

Vanessa bit her lip. She didn't want to lie, but she also didn't want to call her family. "Most of my family lives in Ohio. My parents are close by, but they're on their anniversary cruise. They won't be back until a few days before Christmas."

"I understand that you don't want to disturb your family—"

Vanessa couldn't stop the irritated grunt that escaped her mouth. "Look, my brothers and sister are great, but they are all super busy. Although they would drop everything in a heartbeat if I asked them to. Which I won't. Maybe I can ask a friend to come and stay with me."

Which she wouldn't.

His narrowed gaze took in her expression. "Uh-huh."

He didn't buy it. She waited for him to tell her what to do. She was so sick of people trying to give her orders. She might have been the baby in her family, but she was almost thirty years old. She didn't need a babysitter.

The image of her shooter came to mind. She shivered, then frowned. She didn't like displaying weakness in front of a relative stranger.

Fortunately, Carter's eyes were on his phone. "Okay, I'm ready. Let's go over what happened after you left the clinic."

She nodded, working to keep her expression smooth. She'd perfected keeping her emotions from showing after her life had begun to spiral out of control. If her parents and her five older siblings had any clue how close to self-destruction she had come, they'd have swooped in to rescue her, and they already tended to overcoddle her, which was oppressive.

"I'll answer what I can."

"What can you tell about the car? Make, model, color?"

"Not much. It was too dark. It could have been black, dark blue, or even dark green. I couldn't see the emblem to tell you the make, and honestly, cars look so similar. It wasn't a small SUV or a sports car. It was a four-door sedan. The kind they don't make anymore."

He tapped away on his phone while she spoke. "That actually does narrow it down, since there are fewer cars like that on the road these days. If you'd said a dark pickup truck, for example, that could refer to every other vehicle on the road."

She huffed a surprised laugh. "You're not wrong."

Three of her four brothers drove trucks. Tanner tended to prefer SUVs, but he was the odd man out.

"Let's keep going. Where were you when you noticed him following you?"

She took him through the entire harrowing ride. By the time she came to crashing against the tree and thinking her shooter would get out of his car to finish the job, her whole body shook, despite her attempt to keep a calm front.

"It's okay, Vanessa. He can't hurt you here." Carter stood and opened the cabinet against the wall. She could see a small pile of spare blankets on a shelf inside. He snagged one and brought it back. She tried to protest when he spread it over her.

"I'm fine. I don't want to make more work for the nurses," she argued. He ignored her.

"They won't mind," he said, cutting his gaze toward her without ceasing his task. "They wouldn't want you chilled, either. And it's not like you can turn up the heat."

Except the chill was in her soul and had nothing to do with room temperature.

After he'd arranged the blanket to his satisfaction, he settled back into the chair next to the bed. "I'm sorry I have to make you relive this."

"I understand. Let's just get through this." The sooner they finished, the sooner dread would stop crawling over her skin.

Carter reached over and covered her hand with his. Startled, both at his action and at the warmth flowing up her arm, she jerked slightly. He patted her hand before removing his own and returning his attention to his phone.

Why was her heart going crazy at such a simple thing? Was it because she hadn't let any man touch her since Nolan had destroyed her trust and used a date-rape drug to convince her to do what she'd sworn she'd never do without marriage, then left her pregnant, refusing to even acknowledge the baby was his?

Inhaling deeply, she focused on Carter's questions. "I never got a good look at him. His eyes were hidden in the dark, and the lower half of his face was covered with something. All I could see were his hands..."

Her voice trailed off.

"What? Did you think of something?"

She shook her head. "I don't know. I feel like there was something I missed. Something important. But I can't think what it was."

"You mean something might have been familiar?"

She shrugged. "I'm not sure."

He stood and stretched. "Do me a favor? If you remember anything, text me."

"My phone—"

"I grabbed your purse from the car when the ambulance arrived. I put it in here the last time I came to check on you." He took two steps closer to the bed, then opened the doors on the small bedside table and removed her small backpack-style purse. "I don't know if your phone is in here, but I didn't see it in the front seat."

She reached out for the bag. She opened the zippered pocket on the side and removed her phone, then raised her eyebrows at him. He dictated his information, and she tapped his number into her phone and hit Save.

Nurse Sabrina entered the room again. "Hi, Vanessa. The doctor said you can go home if you have someone to stay with."

She sighed. "Okay. Give me those papers."

Carter's eyebrows rose. When the nurse didn't question her but left the room, those eyebrows lowered into a stern line straight across his forehead. "I thought you said your family was unavailable to stay with you. Do you have a roommate?"

She shook her head. "I don't. But I also refuse to remain

in here. I'll be fine. I've been living on my own for years. And I have neighbors."

His expression darkened. "Vanessa, be reasonable—"

She snarled, "Don't. Tell. Me. That."

He sighed. "I'll let you change. How are you getting home?"

She waved her phone at him. "I'll see if I can get an Uber."

His mouth tightened. "There's a killer after you. He obviously knew your car. And since you may have recognized his voice, and something about him appeared familiar, it's likely he knows you well enough to know where you live."

Fear swamped her. She swallowed.

"I don't have anyone I can call," she finally admitted.

"I have an idea."

Something told her that whether or not she liked his idea didn't matter. She was out of options.

Carter knew determination when he saw it. Vanessa Hall was a prime example. She was independent, feisty and full of grit. He admired that.

He also knew she had a target on her. While he didn't doubt her ability to fend for herself in normal circumstances, she was going against an assailant who was armed.

"Do you have a permit to carry?"

"I don't own a gun. Although I do know how to shoot." She sighed. "I have two brothers in law enforcement. If one of them were around, I'd call them. But Tanner is working a case near Indiana, and Sebastian is in Oregon on a hunting trip."

At least she knew how to use a gun. Still, if she didn't have access to a firearm, if a gunman came after her, she'd have no way to defend herself. He wouldn't leave her helpless, not if he could help it. What he needed to do was create an argument she'd listen to.

"I don't want to tell you what to do. However, you need protection. We have no leads on this shooter, and in less than twelve hours, he's killed a woman and nearly succeeded in killing you. I wouldn't be doing my job if I didn't make your safety a priority."

Her head flopped back against the pillow. She stared up at the ceiling, a tiny pucker forming in the center of her forehead. He ignored the sudden urge to brush his finger over the ridges and smooth out the skin.

Irritated by the inappropriate thought, he took a half step back from her hospital bed.

Folding his arms across his chest, he waited. Finally, she sighed and met his eyes.

"What exactly do you have in mind?"

"Until we come up with a better option, I think our best choice is for me to stay at your place. It's the only way I can protect you." *Since you're going to be stubborn.*

She didn't like it. Every muscle tensed. He waited for the argument.

"Fine," she huffed.

She wasn't pleased, but he'd take the win.

"Good. I'll step out in the hall while you get dressed."

He wasn't waiting for her to change her mind. In the hall, he called his chief. Chief Kaiser picked up almost immediately.

"Yes, Carter?"

"Chief, the hospital is releasing Vanessa to go home. I'm going to go and crash on her couch to keep an eye on her, at least for the night."

The chief hummed into the phone. He could picture her sitting behind her desk, her eyebrows climbing her forehead. Then she surprised him. "I'd say that's for the best. We're stretched a little thin due to the weather, but I think I can have a car do a drive-by every two hours."

It wasn't much, but it was still better than nothing.

"Understood. I'll call you if there are any developments."

He disconnected the call just as the door swung open and Vanessa stood framed in the doorway, her face pale with fatigue and her blue eyes lined with pain.

He pushed away from the wall he'd been leaning on and tried not to focus on the dried bloodstains on her clothing. "Are you set? How do you feel?"

"Like I've been shot."

The little joke fell flat between them.

She sighed. "My shoulder hurts. My head aches where it hit the steering wheel. And I want to burn these clothes."

She gestured awkwardly toward the blood splattered on her sweater and the hole in her winter coat.

He didn't blame her. But they had other things to do first. "Let's get you home. Do you have a prescription?"

"I have two. One for a full-strength pain reliever, which I don't plan on taking. And an antibiotic. Which I will take. They gave me a couple of samples to get me through until tomorrow when the pharmacy opens."

They headed toward the elevator. "I don't blame you about the pain meds. I had a prescription for them once. One pill knocked me out for hours."

"Yeah. For me, even if I don't sleep, they make me feel like I'm moving in slow motion. I don't like not being able to think clearly."

Especially when there's a killer stalking you. He kept that thought to himself. They didn't say another word while they walked through the hospital. At the exit, he nearly asked her to wait while he brought the car around, but she didn't give him the chance. She strode out into the snow, her long legs eating the distance between the door and the parking lot. He kept pace easily. It wasn't often he met a woman who matched him for height. He was five-eleven in his stocking feet. She had to be five-eight or nine, at least.

A thick layer of snow had blanketed the lot since he'd arrived. Their boots crunched on the blue salt crystals covering the ground. The lights had all come on in the parking lot and on the street. It looked pretty, but he knew from experience they were in for a treacherous drive.

He let her into his car and started the engine so the vehicle could warm up while he cleared away the snow. It didn't take long. Heat was just beginning to pour from the vents when he folded his lanky frame into the driver's seat.

His stomach grumbled. "I'm hungry. Why don't we hit a drive-through and then we'll head to your house. Sound okay?"

"I won't argue against that. I never got lunch today."

"Anything I should know of?"

She shook her head. "The only thing I'm allergic to are bees. I'm not a picky eater. Whatever you want will work for me. Unless you go for veal or liver."

He mock shuddered in agreement. "No problem."

He found the nearest fast-food restaurant and got them both burgers and fries. By agreement, they both got bottled water to drink.

She gave him directions to her home. To pass the time, he asked her some casual questions about her job and her family.

"Six kids in your family? Wow. That must have been something. There was only ever me and my baby sister." He pressed his lips together. The one thing he never talked about, not with anyone, was Gretta.

He glanced over and caught the tail end of an odd look

sneaking across her features. But she didn't ask him about his sister. Thankfully.

"That's my house. You know, if you check it out, I'm sure I'll be okay."

"Yeah. No, I'm sleeping on your couch. You need your rest to heal. You won't get that if you aren't able to sleep because you're worried about every sound."

"I won't—"

He cut her off. "After all that's happened today, we know there's a kidnapping or illegal adoption ring in the heart of our town, and like it or not, you are a possible witness, especially if you remember where you heard that voice before. You're an obstacle between the kidnappers and a lot of money. I'm not leaving you alone. At least not tonight."

She turned her head away. He thought that maybe she would refuse to talk with him again. She proved him wrong a second later, her voice coming out soft next to him. "You're right. I wouldn't sleep well. I appreciate it. And I'll accept your offer. But only for tonight."

"Deal."

Hopefully by tomorrow, they'd have whoever had shot her behind bars. Otherwise, he'd have to renege on the bargain he'd just made. Whether she liked it or not, he was now honor-bound to see to it that Vanessa Hall came through this ordeal alive.

Carter pulled into her driveway and stopped the car in front of her garage. A motion light flipped on, flooding the inside of the car with a yellowish glow.

"How do you normally enter the house?"

"Through the door in the garage. I can open it with a passcode."

"Perfect. What is it?"

"Zach. That's the name of one of my brothers."

He nearly rolled his eyes. "We should change that. Zach is something someone who knows you can figure out."

"I will."

He left the car running, then ran over and entered the password. The motorized door hummed and jolted, opening at a snail's pace. His neck prickled. Holding his Glock so anyone watching would have a clear view of it, he turned in a slow circle, scanning the dark horizon. When he saw nothing that sent up red flags in his mind, he returned to the cruiser to open her door.

He used his body as a shield.

"Why didn't you pull in? It might snow again tonight."

"I thought if the killer came by, seeing a police car in your driveway might be a deterrent." He stepped away from the door to give her room to move, still guarding her. And he wanted them to know he hadn't left. "It's slick out here. Do you need help?"

"No. I'll let you know if I change my mind."

Once the door between the house and the garage had been closed behind them and locked, he did a thorough sweep of the entire house. Her single-floor, two-bedroom house had no basement, so it took about five minutes to look over the entire place.

"You're good," he announced, returning to the kitchen. She looked about ready to keel over. "Look, you've had a long day. I just need a blanket. Then you can go to bed. Chief Kaiser will have an officer drive down your street every two hours, and I'll check around every other hour."

He suspected if she hadn't been so completely done in, Vanessa may have argued with him. Instead, she got him a blanket and a pillow, then went into the bedroom. The moment her bedroom door closed, he grabbed his phone.

"Huh. Eleven o'clock already." No wonder he felt like he'd

been walloped by a train. He texted his chief to give her an update. Within two minutes, she replied.

Roberts driving down street now.

Carter walked to the window and peered out in time to catch a glance of the police SUV moving slowly past the house. Good. Everything was secure. Returning to the couch, he set his alarm for an hour.

Settling into sleep proved impossible. Carter's mind was a continual replay loop. Over and over, he went through the day, but no matter how many times he went over all that happened, he still came no closer to finding answers to any of the questions he had.

At 12:00 a.m., his mom started texting him. Brutal messages. She hated her night nurse. He was a horrible son. Why couldn't he have died instead of Gretta? He stopped reading them, knowing that if she was in any distress, Nora, her nurse, would contact him. Although, he did send Nora a text telling her what her patient was doing. His mom wasn't supposed to have her phone unsupervised. In her mental state, it wasn't safe.

Frustrated, he shoved himself off the couch. He might as well do his safety check early. He looked in on Vanessa first. She had sprawled across her bed. It looked like she'd managed to change her blouse and put on a sweater, but she was still in her jeans from before. A little concerned, he moved in closer, listening. The sound of her soft breathing eased his worry. She was fine, but she must have been exhausted. He knew how that felt. Shaking his head in sympathy, he backed away from the bed, careful not to make a sound. She needed her rest.

He closed the door behind him, then went from room to

room. When he reached the kitchen, a sound from above was his only warning.

The shadows on the wall showed something dropping. Agony exploded in the back of Carter's head.

Mandy's killer was in the house, he thought, before losing consciousness.

FOUR

A persistent high-pitched beeping cut through the fog in her exhausted mind. Vanessa bolted upright, confused. What was going on? She was disoriented for a few precious seconds before she understood what the significance of the sound.

The smoke alarm! Thrusting her blankets aside, she swung her legs over the side of the bed. The motion pulled on the stitches in her shoulder, reminding her of all the horrors from earlier.

It also reminded her that Lieutenant Carter Flint was sleeping on her couch. Why hadn't he awakened her?

Dread crawled inside her stomach. Would she find him passed out? Or worse, dead, on her living-room carpet?

She couldn't escape out her window and leave him to his fate. She had to be smart. At some point, she'd need to call 911. She ran back to her bedside table and ripped the phone away from the charging cable. At least she was still in her jeans, so she had a pocket to carry the device in. Thrusting it into her back pocket, she hurried back to the door.

What now? Smoke rose. Dropping to her hands and knees, she ignored the pain pulsing through her shoulder and the ache in her head. Fortunately, her jeans provided a barrier so she didn't scrape her knees on the hardwood floor. She placed her open palm flat against the door. It wasn't hot. Yet.

She opened the door. A slight smoky haze floated over her head. Her nostrils flared at the odor.

Where was Carter?

The light above the kitchen sink was on, creating a beacon and keeping the house from being in total darkness. She had the light on a timer. It was an LED light that went on every night at ten.

She'd never been more grateful for Tanner's insistence on having it until this moment. At the same time, she fumed at herself for not having an alarm system set up to notify the authorities, like her parents had.

She crawled down the hallway, breathing as shallowly as possible. She didn't want to inhale the deadly vapors. She headed toward the kitchen, wincing as she passed beneath the smoke alarm. From the doorway of the kitchen, she'd have a clear view of the couch, where Carter had settled.

It took her less than thirty seconds to crawl the distance, but her knees were starting to protest. She halted in the doorway. Warmth brushed her face. No flames were visible, but the roar behind the door leading to the garage informed her where the flames were. In the center of the room, Carter was sprawled face down. The light created a halo in the room, outlining a small puddle of blood on the floor.

Vanessa gasped. Someone had killed him because he had protected her.

When the prone man groaned, her heart sped up. He was alive. But they'd both die, either from the fire or smoke inhalation, if she didn't find a way to get him out of the house.

She stood, then dashed to the drawer next to the sink and yanked it open. Dipping in both hands, she randomly grabbed handfuls of dishtowels. She sucked in a lungful of air and held her breath before dropping down in front of the door. Jamming towels along the bottom of the door, she used her fingertips to shove the fabric under the gap as much as possible. Her fingers trembled. Every second she spent was another second the fire continued to grow.

The inflow of smoke ceased. Shuddering with relief that the makeshift dam had worked, Vanessa backed away from the door and returned to Carter. They needed to move, now. Once they were safe, she'd call 911 and see if her house could be salvaged.

Moving to Carter's side, she quickly checked him over for injuries. Blood dripped from the back of his head. That would explain why there was so much blood. Head wounds always bled fiercely.

Gently, she shook his shoulder and called his name. When he didn't react, she raised her voice to a shout. "Carter! Wake up! The house is on fire!"

An eerie sound reached her ears from outside the kitchen window. Someone laughing. It was faint. Glancing up, she saw a man, his face covered, staring in at her. She screamed, terror pinging around inside, every nerve end flaring to life.

The man laughed, a chillingly pleasant laugh. "Goodbye, Vanessa."

She barely heard the words through the closed window.

All doubt that the killer knew who she was and had targeted her evaporated. He sank out of sight. Alarms went off in her head. He didn't try to shoot her, or make sure she was dead. He'd set the fire, that was clear, but she remained mobile and able to function.

A cold sweat broke out on her brow, certainty forming in her soul. The back-door entrance was blocked by the flames. That meant she could exit through the front door, right?

Leaving Carter where he was, she sprinted through the living room to the front door. She reached for the doorknob. Her hand closed on nothing. The doorknob was gone. She tried pushing her fingers through the holes to pry open the door. Nothing.

Somehow, he'd sealed the front door closed.

They were trapped inside a burning house.

Oh, no they weren't. She grabbed her phone and dialed 911. She hadn't had to use 911 in years, and now she'd called the number three times in under twenty-four hours. She pushed aside the thought.

"Nine-one-one. What is your emergency?" Then the dispatcher seemed to notice the caller ID. She gasped. "Vanessa? Is that you?"

Vanessa sobbed when she heard the familiar voice. Anyone who didn't know her would think this was a prank call. But Darlene and Vanessa had been friends since high school. Best friends, even.

Although not even Darlene knew her darkest secret.

"Darlene! I'm so glad it's you. Listen. Lieutenant Carter Flint is at my home. He'd been staying here to stand guard because someone tried to kill me earlier. He's been injured, a head injury, and is unconscious. My garage is on fire, and someone has somehow blocked my front door."

Already, she heard Darlene's fast-typing fingers clicking away. "I'm calling for the fire department and police!"

She wasn't waiting around to be rescued. Sooner or later, that fire would break through. Already, the roaring sounded louder and the room temperature seemed to have increased by ten degrees. After placing the phone on speaker, she set it on the floor and ran back to Carter.

She needed to drag him from the room. It would be easier if he was on his back. Grunting with the effort, she rolled him over. She didn't want to drag him by his feet. Bumping his head along the floor could severely injure him, or worse.

She shouted his name again before squatting down to grab

him under his arms. For a wiry man, he was hefty. Probably all those muscles.

She finally budged him a few inches, then another few. It was a slow process. Her shoulder protested. She'd probably ripped out her stitches, but if they survived, she didn't care.

"Vanessa! Help is on the way," Darlene's voice announced over the phone.

"Okay!" she gasped. Then stopped talking. She couldn't pull a full-grown man and hold a conversation at the same time.

Please, please, let someone arrive soon.

The window on the door to the garage shattered. Smoke poured in through the hole.

Vanessa shrieked once, then yanked on Carter, desperation giving her the drive to pull him the rest of the way from the kitchen to the dining room. His uniform slid smoothly along the wooden floor. She edged him inch by inch into the living room. Her goal was the picture window. If she could get there and break it, it was large enough and low enough to the ground that she might, maybe, be able to push him through. And hopefully, have enough time to jump through after him.

"Vanessa!"

She heard Darlene shout, but didn't have enough oxygen to respond. The smoke in the air was choking her.

Carter groaned, twisting in her grasp, pulling away from her. She felt the stitches in her shoulder give and blood trickled from her injured shoulder. It wouldn't matter if both of them died here.

Her strength gone, she slumped on the floor next to him, coughing.

Would they be alive when help arrived? Or would Mandy's killer claim two more lives?

* * *

Pain wracked his body. His head was on fire.

Wait. Fire. Smoke tainted the air he was breathing. Near him, there a wracking cough. Forcing open his eyelids, Carter rolled onto his side. He couldn't keep a groan down. His pain wasn't his main concern, though.

Vanessa lay collapsed on the floor next to him, coughing, tears rolling down her pale cheeks. Blood dotted the shoulder of her light blue sweater. His eyes watered from the smoke.

"Vanessa," he croaked, his throat parched from the smoke and the steadily increasing heat. "We need to move."

"Door blocked," she responded, her voice hoarse. "Need to break the window."

He glanced back. A wall of flames had obliterated the door to the garage. They had minutes before the kitchen went up. After that, it would be the dining room and living room. That she had blinds instead of drapes would slow it down. As would the fact that it was wood flooring. If she had carpet, they'd have no hope.

He got to his hands and knees, then up to a squat, staying below the smoke.

He wasn't sure what she meant by the door being blocked. From where he was crouching, it looked fine. But he had to trust her judgment, knowing she would have investigated before he woke up.

"Let's get closer to the window. Farther from the fire."

She lifted one hand to show she heard and understood, but continued to cough. He helped her up and wrapped his left arm around her waist. She did the same with her right arm. It was hard to say who was leaning on who. With his head wound leaving him wobbly and her constant coughing, the two of them stumbled toward the large picture window. They nearly toppled over once. He slammed his arm against the china cabinet as he caught them. It shook ominously, the dishes inside rattling.

"Grandma's dishes," she murmured.

The glow of the streetlamp beckoned them toward the window. Snowflakes danced temptingly in the light's aura. Outside the range of the beam, the night remained pitch-black.

A few more feet. They were so close.

Carter's lungs ached with the need to breathe. Lifting his free arm, he pressed his mouth and nose against the fabric to filter out as much of the smoke as possible and sucked in a deep breath. Then he held it again and took three more steps toward the window.

They staggered forward until they stood within three feet of their goal. Without warning, Vanessa stumbled to her knees, coughing and gagging. Carter encouraged her to rise, feeling his own legs wobble under the strain to keep upright. His vision blurred. Whether from the smoke-filled air or from his head injury, he didn't know. He refused to give in to the urge to sink down and rest. If they didn't make it to the window in time, they were going to die right here.

He grabbed her under both arms, then heaved her back to her feet. She cried out. He winced, knowing he was putting pressure on her injured shoulder. It couldn't be helped. He'd rather cause her a little pain now, then be gentle and allow her to perish in the fire consuming the walls behind them.

He glanced over his shoulder. The kitchen was fully engulfed. The doorway was an arch of glowing flames. The china cabinet on the wall next to the door began to smolder. Soon, it, too, would be burning. The cell phone that had been sitting on the floor was toast, the case warped and melting.

Carter bent down, lifted Vanessa into his arms and slung

her over his shoulders. He carried her the rest of the way toward the window.

"Hold on, Vanessa." He set her on her feet. She swayed. He helped her back down on the floor. "I'm going to break this window. Once I do, the incoming oxygen will feed the flames. Stay down, but when I tell you to go, we need to move. Stay with me."

"I will," she promised in a rusty voice.

Behind him, the flames raced up the wall. Sweat dripped down the back of his neck. He picked up a chair and threw it at the window. Glass shattered, the sound almost immediately swallowed up by the bellow of oxygen hitting the burning wood mere feet away from them.

Carter removed his uniform jacket and swept the glass off the base of the window frame. Vanessa crawled deeper into the room.

"Vanessa, wait!"

She returned a second later with a throw from the couch. Together, they settled it on the windowsill. Then he picked her up and gently dropped her out the opening. She landed on the snow below and fell into the hedge of bushes.

The back of his leg began to sting. He looked away from Vanessa. His pant leg burned. The acrid smell of the polyester-and-wool blend smoldering hit his nostrils.

He was out of time.

Covering his head with his arms, he dove through the window. Hitting the ground, he rolled on the cold snow until his uniform was no longer on fire.

"Are you alright?"

He turned at Vanessa's voice. The light cast a silver silhouette around her, illuminating her magnificent hair, but leaving her blue eyes in deep shadows. "I've been better. Did I hear someone on the phone?"

"I called nine-one-one," she croaked, then spluttered into a coughing fit. "Sorry."

She rubbed her eyes with the palms of her hands.

He glanced around. Where were the fire engines? Or the police?

Then, he grimaced. Vanessa lived outside of the city limits. The paid department that served the city didn't service the rural areas. Some of the rural volunteer fire departments were low on members. If they didn't get a response from the local department, they'd have to expand the call to the next volunteer fire department over.

But what was keeping the police?

"Let's sit in my car while we wait," he suggested.

He assisted Vanessa up from the ground. Now that they were in the cold air, her coughing had slowed down. Cold air could be tricky. If it was too cold, it could exacerbate the problem. On the other hand, sometimes cooler air helped ease tight air passages.

She gasped, her eyes growing wider in the light.

But the light had been behind her.

Alarmed, he half spun to look at the house they'd just escaped. Through the broken window, a wall of fire met his horrified gaze. Instinctively, he tightened his grip on her waist. She balanced against him. A single whimper snuck out. Then she said, "Please. Your car?"

He nodded. And gently turned them back to the lone vehicle in the driveway.

Together, they hobbled in the direction of his waiting cruiser. It had never been more appealing. The moment he got in, he'd turn it on and get the heat up and running.

Carter guided her around to the passenger-side door and opened it.

A bullet hit the back of his vehicle, smashing the passenger taillight.

"Get down!"

Carter shoved Vanessa into the cruiser and slammed the door. She curled up on the floorboard in front of the seat until her head sank below the window. Whipping out his weapon, Carter crouched and hurried around to the driver's side, his eyes scanning the area. Backup hadn't arrived yet. He couldn't stay here and risk leaving Vanessa vulnerable.

A second shot hit the side of the cruiser. Carter ducked inside, got behind the wheel and started the engine.

A third bullet dinged the driver's-side door.

Had they escaped the fire only to be murdered in the driveway?

FIVE

•

Carter yanked the gearshift into Reverse and barreled backward out of the driveway. The rear tires skidded off the gravel and churned up the snow. They bumped over the curb so hard his teeth clicked.

He barely allowed the cruiser to stop before hurling it into Drive. "Don't get up yet," he warned Vanessa.

He tried to locate the shooter, but couldn't see anyone hiding in the darkness. After he squealed around the corner, he relaxed.

"I think it's safe."

For now.

He jabbed his finger at the call button and dialed the station to report in.

Next to him, Vanessa pulled herself off the floorboard and crawled into the passenger seat. The seat belt clicked. He frowned. In the dim light, the spots of blood had spread over her shoulder. She needed to go back to the hospital.

"Chief Kaiser, here."

Carter blinked. He'd been expecting one of the officers to answer. The chief wasn't scheduled to arrive this early today.

"Hello?"

"Oh, sorry, Chief, it's Carter."

"Carter!" the chief responded. "Where's Vanessa? I heard fire trucks and an ambulance are on the way to your location."

"Vanessa's here." He thought over what she said. "We're heading away from the scene. The house is fully involved. There's an active shooter on the premises. I need backup."

"Sergeant Roberts should be there," Chief replied. "He responded to the original dispatch and said he was only three miles away and would be there within five minutes. That was almost half an hour ago."

The hair on his arms stood on end. "He never showed up."

Carter flicked his eyes to the clock on the dashboard. "He never did his last drive-by. He would have been on his way back for that."

Something was definitely not adding up. Roberts was just about the most reliable cop he'd ever met. If he was late, there was an issue.

"I don't like this," the chief stated, echoing his sentiments. "I'm sending out more police backup."

"I need to get Vanessa medical care, Chief."

"Smoke inhalation?" she asked, guessing.

"Possibly," he informed his boss. "And I suspect she's reopened her wound."

Vanessa's eyes shot to her shoulder. When she saw the blood, she took her hand and pressed it against the wound.

The road stretched out dark and empty ahead of him. He drove past house after house without seeing any sign of life, outside of the occasional Christmas lights in the yard or a lit tree in the window. Probably on a timer.

His radio crackled to life. The fire engines had arrived on the scene. He heard the words *total loss* and winced. Vanessa groaned.

"I'm sorry."

The words were inadequate, but he couldn't think of anything else to say. Houses and personal possessions meant zero when compared to a person's life. But it still hurt to see a part of your life destroyed.

She swiped her hands across her eyes. "I'm in shock, I think. I've lived there since my grandmother died six years ago. That was her house."

That made it even worse.

"I'm so angry," she whispered, shame creeping into the soft tones.

He nodded. "Not surprising. Someone tried to kill you. Twice."

"This is going to sound strange, but the fact that he destroyed my grandma's house is what I can't get past."

"You're a nurse."

"Your point?"

"My point is I know you're aware that people sometimes focus on the less urgent stuff until they can face the really harsh realities."

He'd done that when his sister died. He'd focused on his job to drown out the anger coming from his mother. The problem was, he'd only put off the inevitable. By the time he'd surfaced from his self-imposed isolation, his mother had begun to show signs of dementia.

Had trauma brought it on?

He didn't know. The doctors said it was possible. They were always learning new things about death. But one thing he did know was that by burying himself in his job, he'd lost precious time with his mom.

The radio beeped again. "Shots fired. Corner of Hill and Grove. Sterling Ridge police department. EMS and ambulance, stage until scene is safe. Active shooter at large. Proceed with caution."

A new voice entered the conversation. Static crackled.

"Sterling Ridge Ambulance responding. All EMS report to Vick's Furniture Store for staging."

A chill raced up his spine.

"That's just a block from my house!" Vanessa blurted, leaning forward in her seat. Her red hair swung like a curtain in front of her face.

"I'm concerned that Roberts hasn't responded. He should be in the area."

The chief called. He picked up on the first ring. "Chief?"

"Carter, did you hear the dispatch?"

"Yes, ma'am. I'm circling back around to take a look." He turned left at the next intersection. Two blocks later, he took another left onto Grove. A new nightmare appeared in front of his eyes. Brian Roberts's vehicle was in the ditch, directly under a streetlamp. "Chief! Brian's cruiser's on the side of the road. Looks like the front wheel is hanging over the ditch."

He allowed himself the small hope that Brian was stuck, and not something darker. But then, why hadn't his friend and colleague called for assistance?

It didn't bode well. Slowing down, he drove alongside Brian's cruiser. The engine was humming. From where he sat, he could see Brian slumped down in his seat. He had seen Vanessa in a similar posture only a few hours before. She had lived.

He refused to think any further. He shifted into Park and reached for his weapon. He needed to be ready if the shooter was out there waiting. They were a block from the fire. He could see the glimmer of lights flashing against the sky of the fire trucks. If the shooter had any self-preservation instincts, he would have already fled the scene.

Still, he needed to be cautious.

"Chief, I'm next to Brian's vehicle. I don't see any sign of the shooter. I don't think he's conscious. I need to go check on him, but I don't want to leave a civilian without protection."

"Stay alert for the shooter, Lieutenant. I have Lieutenant Talbot on the way to your location. The roads are dicey. The ambulance is on the way, too."

"Understood. I'm not leaving the vehicle, but I do need to step outside to get a good look around." He turned to Vanessa. "Wait here." He glanced around. "And I hate to say it, get down again."

She didn't argue, but slid back down.

"I'm getting out now."

"Be careful, Lieutenant. The moment you see danger, you get the civilian to safety."

He didn't like the plan. Leaving a fellow officer went against the grain. But he knew Vanessa's safety was the priority. "I will, Chief."

Stepping out of the cruiser, he made a slow turn, his gun pointed down, slightly in front of him.

Lights swirled around him. Carter's breath whooshed out of him in relief. Brett had arrived to provide backup. A second officer climbed out with him.

"Talbot's here. He brought Crouse."

"Good. Now, please go and check on Roberts and let me know his condition," she ordered, her voice taut with tension.

He waved Brett and Crouse over.

"Crouse, I need you to stay with my vehicle. I have a civilian inside."

"Yes, sir."

The two lieutenants made their way to the downed colleague.

The moment Brett shone his flashlight into the car, Carter's heart sank. The sergeant's chest was covered with a large stain.

Brett jiggled the door handle.

The sergeant's head flopped in their direction. His eyes opened and he peered blearily at them.

Carter ran back to the cruiser. "Chief! He's alive. Shot in the chest but alive."

"I hear you. The paramedics are coming on the scene now."

After hanging up with his chief, he glanced at Vanessa.

"How are you holding up?"

She shrugged one shoulder. "Okay, I guess. Why would he shoot a cop?"

He'd wondered about that. "Brian must have interrupted him. Or maybe he saw him. I don't know. Either way, I'm crossing my fingers that Brian saw the shooter. You okay for a few minutes? Officer Crouse here will stay with you."

"Don't worry about me. I'll be fine. You do your job."

"I'll keep her safe, sir." Crouse lifted his head and met Carter's gaze. Carter nodded and returned to wait with Brett.

When the ambulance pulled in a few minutes later, Brett and Carter stood guard while the other officer was checked over and loaded into the ambulance.

One of the paramedics gave both Carter and Vanessa a cursory look over. "You should come to the hospital and get checked out, the two of you. You might have a concussion and she should get her wound restitched."

"Can't she go with you now?"

"No room."

Carter ran a hand through his hair. He huffed a tired sigh. "Fine. I'll bring her to the hospital myself."

It wasn't that he minded. But his head ached and he was exhausted. But there was nothing else he could do.

They'd go and get checked out.

Man, he hated going to hospitals. Every time he entered

one, he was smacked in the face with memories of receiving a hysterical call from his mother in the middle of a shift, then rushing to the hospital, only to learn his sister had already died.

"I'll wait here until the crime-scene unit arrives, then I'll go and see what the fire chief says," Brett told him before sauntering to his own cruiser, where he'd be warm.

Carter sketched a brief wave then got back into the front seat. "We'll head to the hospital. Then I need to figure out where we can stay to keep you safe," he said to Vanessa.

He didn't want to mention the fact that her home was gone, but they couldn't ignore the truth. She had a killer after her and needed to find shelter. Fast.

"I don't want to go to the hospital."

He pulled away from Brian's cruiser. The chief would take care of getting it back to the station. It was part of a crime scene now, so he didn't want to touch it.

"I'm sorry, but you need to. You've stopped coughing but your wound is still opened. You need to get it restitched."

"I don't think I can go." Her soft voice shook, but he could tell she meant what she said. "Someone is out to kill me—someone I obviously know. He knows where I work. Where I live...lived. He can be anyone and I wouldn't know. I won't feel safe anywhere until he's caught."

He wanted to argue with her, except a tiny voice inside his head told him she might be correct. And if she wasn't safe at the hospital, just where would she be safe?

Vanessa's head ached. Her chest ached. In fact, she'd be hard pressed to think of a muscle that didn't. She'd endured an incredible amount of trauma in the past few hours.

That didn't alter her determination to avoid the hospital.

"Vanessa."

His voice breaking into the silence startled her. He'd sat without talking for the past ten minutes, no doubt trying to figure out how to convince her to change her mind. Her name sounded like a caress coming from his lips.

She shook her head. She was not attracted to him. She had her life planned out, and a man, any man, played no part in it. She'd been betrayed before, and that was enough. She would protect her vulnerable heart from abuse. She was a strong, intelligent woman with a satisfying career. That had been enough for a long time.

Why did it suddenly feel so empty?

"Vanessa?"

"Oh, sorry. I was woolgathering." She glanced at the clock. "I can't believe it's only five in the morning."

It had been two hours since they escaped her burning house. The streetlight and the vehicle's instrument panel provided some light. Enough to see the concern on his face. She's been the cause of his worry.

Carter shifted in his seat. "Look, I understand what you're saying. But I can stay with you."

She shook her head, primed to argue before he finished his statement. "I don't want to risk it. No, I won't go to the hospital. I'll contact the clinic and call off from work today. After yesterday, no one would expect me to go in. And I'll lay low for a while."

Although where she'd go, she had no idea. She could probably call her sister-in-law, Fran. But she didn't want to bring this trouble into Fran's home. She and her brother Tanner had just adopted three-year-old twins. She'd never forgive herself if her attacker followed her to Sutter Springs, Ohio, and injured Fran or those sweet little boys.

No, she was on her own with this one. She snuck a glance at Carter.

He'd clenched his jaw. She waited. Finally, he unglued his jaw enough to respond. "I don't like it. You've opened your wound..."

His phone rang, cutting off his litany of complaints. The words *The Chief* flashed on dashboard. He hit the button to accept the call. She scooted back into her seat and fumbled with the seat belt until it buckled. Such a simple task had been complicated by her injury. Her shoulder protested and her entire body ached like she'd been run over by a truck. Weariness settled over her like a blanket. All she wanted was to crawl into a hole somewhere and sleep for a month.

Tears stung her eyes. No. What she wanted was her mother. Her mother, who was in the middle of the ocean with her dad. They'd saved for this cruise for the past three years. She couldn't ask them to cut their cruise short.

Not yet.

"Yes, Chief?" Carter turned up the volume.

"I just got off the phone with Brett. Sergeant Roberts is in surgery now. I will keep you posted on the sergeant's condition."

"Thanks, Chief." Carter cleared his throat. "I thought it strange that someone willing to kill would miss his target several times in a row."

"What do you mean? He killed Mandy," Vanessa said, then flushed. "Sorry. Didn't mean to interrupt a police call."

"That's alright, Miss Hall," the Chief replied. "I want to hear more about what Carter is thinking, too."

"Yes, someone killed Mandy. But he missed you, Vanessa, then he missed us again when we were at your house, and he failed to mortally wound Brian."

"He has trouble with moving targets," the chief mused.

"Exactly. I don't know how that helps us, except it takes anyone with significant skills off the list of suspects."

"Could be. Although, we might not know their skill level. So it may be a moot point."

"Right, and he could kill someone accidentally. Stray bullets hit moving targets every day."

That wasn't comforting. Vanessa listened to their conversation but didn't add any more to it. It chilled her to her very soul to hear people talking so calmly about someone getting killed. But even though they talked without emotion, she had seen Carter's face when he thought his fellow officer might be dead.

A minute later, Carter disconnected the call with his chief. He sent Vanessa a questioning glance.

"You holding on?"

"Yeah." Barely.

His strong arms braced on the wheel. "Did you pay attention to the end of my chat with my boss?"

"Sorry. I tuned out for a few minutes. Did I miss something?"

"Maybe." He turned a corner. She could see that they were moving closer to town. "I told the chief that I'll be doing work from home today. She doesn't want me coming in, seeing as we were just in a fire and I got my head bashed pretty good. I made a compromise. Since we are not at full capacity, I'll continue to work at my house. My mom, who has been diagnosed with dementia and now lives in my house, is being cared for by her cousin today. I made those plans yesterday when I knew I'd be staying at your place."

She tried to grasp what he was telling her, but so far, it was going completely over her head. "I still don't—"

Carter pulled the car into a driveway and hit the garage-door opener on the sun visor. When the door opened, he moved the cruiser inside. "Usually, I leave the cruiser outside, because who'd mess with the police, right? But I think we need to keep the fact that you're with me quiet."

After shutting off the engine, Carter slipped from the car before she had time to ask any more questions. He jogged around the car to her side.

When he opened the door, she slowly unfolded her sore frame from the vehicle. "I thought you'd insist I go to the hospital to get my shoulder taken care of."

"Well, I can't force you," he told her, leading her into the house. "Come on. I know you need to rest."

She followed him in, confused. He pointed to an island with a high countertop in the center of the room. Four chairs lined one side. "Go ahead and grab a seat. I'll be right back."

She slid onto a chair and wilted against the back. All she wanted was two ibuprofen and a soft bed. It wouldn't hurt to close her eyes for just a minute while she waited. She allowed her lids to close and sank her head down on her arms, folded on the cool tabletop.

"Vanessa? Hey, Vanessa?"

Startled, she jolted upright. "What happened?"

"You fell asleep." Carter stood next to her, his gray eyes searching her face with concern.

She jerked her gaze from his, mortified, and noticed a tackle box in front of her.

"Are you going fishing?"

He chuckled. She shivered.

"Nope. That's my first-aid kit. I'm going to look at your shoulder and—" he held up a box of Dermabond surgical glue "—I'm going to tend to it if necessary."

She blinked. "You can't do that. You're not trained."

He flashed a half smile at her. "Actually, I am. I was trained prior to an undercover mission last year. I still have the supplies I need. That's why I didn't fuss too hard when you refused to go to the hospital."

He held up a black tank shirt. "I thought you can change into this."

She wanted to say "no, thank you." But that wouldn't be the wise course of action. She grabbed the offered shirt, went into the bathroom and changed, then returned to find him waiting, latex gloves already on his hands.

A few seconds later, she bit her lip to keep from crying out as he recleaned the wound. "Why would the doctor use actual stitches?"

She might have smiled at his snarly tone if it hadn't hurt so much. "Some doctors don't trust the glue, I guess."

He grunted, then removed the broken stitches before sealing the wound. Within moments, he'd applied a clean bandage. "This should hold it. At least we won't need to worry about it breaking open again."

When she reached for her sweater again, he looked at her back. She froze, knowing what he'd seen. Her tattoo.

A butterfly, with two blue wings and two pink ones. The bottom wings looked like a baby rattle. Maybe he wouldn't put two and two together.

Suddenly, the secret she'd carried alone for so long felt too big. "I got that in college. I had a miscarriage."

"Vanessa, I'm sorry."

"Thanks." She glanced down at her hands. "No one else knows."

It felt important that he know it wasn't something she talked about. She couldn't say she was over it. Because she wasn't. She thought about the child she'd almost had every day. Never knowing if it were a girl or a boy.

He didn't ask questions.

Instead, he showed her a bedroom where she could rest.

"You can sleep in here for as long as you need to. I have an alarm system. I'll be in the living room, working, if you need me."

She started to turn away from him, then looked back. "Thank you, Carter. I don't think I would have survived without you."

He shrugged and gave her a smile.

"I hate to ask for anything else. But I need to pick up my antibiotic."

"Of course. When you wake up, we'll head out and get it."

She scurried into the room and closed the door, her heart pounding. She'd told him about the baby. No one except her and Nolan had ever known about her baby. Not even her best friend, Darlene, and definitely not her parents or siblings.

And now, Carter, a man nearly a stranger, knew she'd had a miscarriage. Hopefully, she wouldn't regret telling him.

Right now, though, she had weightier problems to worry about. Like finding the criminal so intent on keeping his identity private that he'd killed Mandy, and nearly killed Sergeant Roberts, Carter and herself.

Only when he was caught, could she return to her life.

SIX

Carter bypassed the coffeepot on his kitchen counter and grabbed an energy drink from the refrigerator. He didn't drink them often. They all tasted like turpentine to him. At the moment, though, he needed the caffeine if he was going to remain alert enough to work, regardless of taste.

After popping open the can, he took a swig and grimaced, giving the coffeepot one last longing glance before heading to the living room. He wanted to watch the news and see the coverage of the fire. He had a small folding table and a wooden chair stashed in the corner for when he needed to work from home.

Carter stationed the table and chair in front of the fireplace, then hit the remote control. He set the volume on low. The Erie news channels broadcast several times during the day, including from 5:00 a.m. until 7:00 a.m., and then again at noon. It was almost 6:00 a.m.

He stifled a yawn. It was going to be a long day. He chugged the energy drink, then set aside the empty can. Maybe after the news, he'd make a pot of very black coffee. It had been a long time since he'd pulled an all-nighter and worked the following day.

Carter opened his laptop and typed in his password. On the TV, the weather anchor reported a lake-effect snow warning in Erie and Crawford Counties until 11:00 a.m. All the schools in the area were closed for the day due to slick roads, white-out conditions and temperatures below zero.

"Windchill of negative fifteen. Brrr. Sounds like a good day to stay inside."

He had another five minutes before the next news segment began. He read through his emails. Brett informed him that Opal Bontrager had safely delivered a baby boy. However, because the child arrived early, he'd spend a week or two in the neonatal intensive care unit, or the NICU. Opal had needed a caesarean section, so she'd be in the hospital for the next few days as well. The local police agreed to provide protection for both the baby and the new mother.

Vanessa would be happy to hear that. She'd been so worried about what would happen to both of them.

Mandy's family had been notified of her death and interviewed. It turned out Mandy had maxed out three credit cards. She was nearly sixty thousand dollars in debt and creditors had started calling her. The young woman desperately needed money.

It still didn't excuse what she'd done. She'd bartered a child and a woman's life to extricate herself from a problem she created. He shook his head. What a waste of a life.

The introductory music for the local news played. Carter pushed aside his laptop and turned the volume up just enough so he could hear it without being loud enough to keep Vanessa awake.

Although, after the night she'd just had, he doubted she'd rest easy.

Five minutes later, the bedroom door opened and Vanessa walked out. She sank down on the couch and curled her legs beneath her. Reaching back, he grabbed the afghan his mother had made years earlier and tossed it to her.

"Thanks." Vanessa snuggled under the blanket and turned her haunted gaze to the TV.

"Did I wake you up?"

"I couldn't sleep. Being in that room by myself made me nervous. Do you mind if I'm here?"

"Of course not." Should he turn off the TV? She probably didn't want to see her house on the news.

Before he could decide, the burning structure was on the screen.

"Police are searching for a gunman who set a neighborhood house on fire and shot an on-duty officer."

Vanessa's sleepy expression vanished in an instant. Shocked, she stared at what was left of her home. It had been completely dark when they'd escaped. Seeing it in the daylight had to be devastating.

Carter's phone dinged. "It's from the chief. Sergeant Roberts is out of surgery. The sergeant is expected to make a full recovery, but he'll be out of commission for at least a couple of months. The bullet missed his heart, but it nicked a lung. The damage was reparable. But still bad. His condition is stable."

"I'm glad he'll recover." She glanced again at the TV.

"The fire started in the garage," the reporter continued. "The fire inspector is on scene to determine what type of accelerant was used. No bottles or cans were left at the scene." Then, the reporter smiled at the camera.

"Those reporters are far too cheerful," Vanessa commented darkly.

"Yes, but that's their job."

"How did he get in to set the fire?" Vanessa shuddered, pulling the Afghan tighter around her. "I don't have a real security system, but if someone were trying to enter a passcode and failed, or tried to break in, it would beep. Surely, one of us would have heard that."

"I was thinking about that. Since this all started last night, it's highly unlikely someone has been watching you. Which means it's probably someone who knows you really well."

"We already said that. It is someone I know."

"I don't mean just that you know them. This is a person who knows enough about you, or has access to your information, to be able to guess your password. Have you told it to anyone else?"

He opened up the notes app on his phone, prepared to make a list of suspects.

She sank her head into her hands, shoving her fingers deep into the red curls.

"What is it?"

Vanessa wiped her face and raised her head. She huffed out a bitter laugh. "Didn't you just say last night that my password was easy to figure out?"

He set down his phone. "I did. You used your brother's name. But how many people here know you have a brother named Zach?"

"A lot of people know. Zach's a surgeon. He worked at the hospital here for years before he took the position of chief of surgery in another hospital. He's one of those guys that seems to know everyone. So, no, I didn't tell anyone. But it wouldn't have been difficult to figure out. Out of all my siblings, he's the one I'm closest to."

Carter tapped a thoughtful finger against his chin. "I'm also considering the option that the killer might have been casing your house and somehow saw me enter the password."

He recalled the feeling that someone might have been watching. He should have called it in. Then he frowned.

"They couldn't have used the door."

She shifted to sit cross-legged on the couch. "Why not?"

"Because there's no way I wouldn't have heard the garage door open. Not only is it loud, but it takes at least twenty seconds. And it was shut, so they'd have had to close it, too."

Vanessa chewed on her lip in thought. "Then they must have picked the lock to the main door. It's in the back of the garage. There's no passcode for that."

He nodded, recalling the door that led from the garage to the backyard. "Getting into the house wouldn't have been a problem. I remember the door leading to the kitchen had been unlocked."

She blew out a breath. "Trust me, if I ever own a house with an attached garage again, which I doubt after this, I will have all the doors locked. I regret not having a full-on security system. Next time, I will. I don't want this to ever happen again."

"Sounds like a good plan. Although, if you have a strong security system, you could probably have an attached garage."

"Nope. I'd be terrified to go in there." She gave him a fleeting smile. One that made his breath hitch in his chest. "I should get a dog. The bigger, the better."

"I've always wanted a dog myself." He stood. "I'm going to make coffee. Want some?"

She unfolded her legs and stood. "Yeah. I don't think I'm going to bed. So why don't you have a dog if you always wanted one?"

They walked side by side into the kitchen. "You forget—my mom lives here. She's allergic to dogs and cats. The only pet we've ever had is fish."

She made a noise at the back of her throat.

"I know. But that's life."

"We always had at least a dog and a cat. Usually more," she added, snickering. "I was forever bringing animals home."

"I'm surprised you didn't have a pet now."

"With my work hours, I didn't feel right leaving a pet alone for so many hours." She paused. "I'd once dreamed of becoming a vet."

He shot a glance her way and immediately knew she regretted revealing that much about herself.

"That's cool," he said casually, then squashed down his curiosity. He didn't need to know about her hopes and dreams.

But he wanted to know. He also wanted to know who or what put that defeated and guarded look in her eyes. He'd never been confrontational. But he had the urge to charge to her defense. But how did one fight against the ghosts of someone else's past?

And even if he knew what had happened to her, it wasn't any of his business. He and Vanessa Hall were acquaintances. Nothing more. He had too many responsibilities, and carried too much emotional baggage, to ever dream of having more with anyone.

He'd never regretted that more than he did at this very moment.

Why had she told him that she'd dreamed of becoming a veterinarian? Carter Flint was the cop protecting her. They weren't a couple. He was nothing to her, and vice versa.

But he did make her feel safe, even after all that had happened in the past twenty-four hours. She knew in her soul that Lieutenant Carter Flint would put himself between her and a bullet. Or whatever danger was hurled at her.

It had been a long time since she'd felt that way.

Mostly because she'd pushed away her family.

Speaking of family. "I should call someone and let them know I'm okay. Just in case they saw the news. If they tried my phone, they wouldn't get an answer since it was destroyed in the fire."

"Good idea. You can use my phone."

He handed it over, then ducked out of the room. She appreciated his tact in giving her privacy. As she dialed the number for her brother Zach, though, she found she could have used Carter's silent support.

She got a message that the number she'd called was temporarily not in service. She frowned. It was only after seven in the morning. Zach was usually driving in to work now. And he was so type A, he'd never let his phone service lapse. Then a light bulb went on in her brain. Zach and his wife, Kathy, had gone away for the week to celebrate both their birthdays, which happened to be two days apart. They'd rented a lodge and had warned that they wouldn't have good service.

She began to dial Tanner. Then stopped. He was also out of town on a case. She certainly didn't want to disturb Fran, who would, she knew, drop everything to come and get her.

And then Vanessa would worry about Fran and the twins' safety until Tanner returned home. Although Fran was officially law enforcement, as a forensic artist she didn't carry a gun. She started to dial Fran's number, then stopped. Fran had the kids at her parents' house for a few days while Tanner was out of town. She doubted they'd see the news there.

She chewed her lip. Logan lived out of state. Sebastian was away bear hunting with his buddies. And her parents were on a cruise.

That left Lillian. She dialed her sister's number. She got Lillian's voice mail. Lillian wouldn't recognize the number. She'd leave a message. "Hey, Lill. It's me, Vanessa. Listen, can you call me back at this number?" She didn't know it and hadn't checked before she'd called. "My phone was destroyed, and I'm using a, um, a friend's. 'Bye."

It did no good to worry. Quickly, remembering she was supposed to work later, she called the clinic and let them know she'd be off today.

"I heard about the accident," Shannon said. "I hope you can rest and feel better."

Vanessa didn't correct her. "Thanks. You know what, can you just mark me off for tomorrow, too? I don't have a car or a phone, so I don't know how to let you know if I can come in. I don't want to leave you shorthanded."

"No problem."

Carter returned a moment later. "All done?"

"Sort of. I called Lillian, my sister. She didn't answer, so I left a voice mail."

The corners of his mouth turned down. His eyebrows lowered. "Does she listen to voice mails? You could send her a text."

"I have no idea if she'll listen to the message." She doubted it. It was an unfamiliar number, and Lillian often ignored voice mails from numbers she didn't know. "She has her phone set up to mark all unknown numbers as spam. So unless you're in her contacts, a text wouldn't help."

"Wow. Okay, so we'll keep to our original plan. Hopefully, she'll contact you soon. Could you try to get her at work?"

She shook her head, embarrassed to admit she didn't have her sister's work number. In fact, Lillian had changed jobs a few times since her son had been born, so Vanessa wasn't even sure where she worked.

When this was over, she'd do better to be involved in her siblings' lives.

"Well, I need to figure out where you'll be safe."

She didn't like the sound of that. "Do you think the kidnapper will try and steal another baby?"

"Absolutely," he responded without hesitation. "Based on

what you overheard, this abduction ring has already sold a baby. He's been paid and needs to supply a newborn soon. I'm afraid we'll be called in to another abduction soon."

"Also, he mentioned another target in the next three months."

Carter handed her a fresh mug of coffee then leaned his hip against the counter. He took a sip. "Milk's in the fridge and sugar is in the cupboard."

She dipped her head in silent thanks, then rummaged around the cupboard and fridge to doctor up her hot drink. He winced when she put a second helping of sugar in the mug. She bit back a grin.

Once her coffee met the approval of her sweet tooth, she returned to their conversation. "I want to help."

He raised one eyebrow. "Oh? What's on your mind?"

She took a sip to steady her nerves. It was foolish to involve herself in police business. But she had expertise he needed to save lives. "I am a certified nurse midwife. I have knowledge of many of the pregnant Amish and Mennonite women in the area."

"But we don't know if his next victim is in the area."

"True, but there aren't very many women who do what I do in this area. While I'm stationed at Sterling Ridge, I do visit patients once a week in LaMar Pond. And I have access to other contacts that might know more about any pregnant Amish and Mennonite women in the area."

"True, but to get any of those other contacts, it might be considered against confidentiality to reveal information. We might not be able to get that."

"If the pregnant women go to a place where I am contracted as a certified nurse midwife, I will be able to access, or learn about, the clients. Because I might be on call when they come in. I also am trusted in the Amish communities nearby. We might be able to talk to those in the area to find out what we need to know. Amish don't typically talk about pregnancy, so it's really our only chance."

She watched him mull over what she'd said and held her breath. If he went and tried and find pregnant Amish women on his own, he'd hit a wall. No one would talk with him. As a rule, the Amish didn't trust the police. Or the government.

"Let me think about it and talk it over with the chief." His intense stare melded with her gaze. Her stomach flipped. "I don't like it. Having a civilian involved, there's danger. But I also don't like leaving you on your own. We are low on numbers with Brian being out, and another officer is on maternity leave. So I'm your protective detail for the moment."

She nodded and let the subject drop.

By lunchtime, the snow outside had eased. A snowplow had gone past Carter's house twice. He'd called his mom's cousin and had made arrangements for his mother to stay there for the next few days.

"I don't want my mom here, where she'll be vulnerable until we catch this shooter and you can go back to your own life."

Wherever that would be. She had no home. She could probably stay with her parents or one of her siblings, once they returned. She could stay with Darlene, except her dear friend was still a newlywed. She'd feel uncomfortable imposing on her.

She'd have to get an apartment soon.

She shuddered. Would she ever feel safe enough to live on her own again?

One o'clock rolled around. Her sister hadn't returned her call. She borrowed Carter's phone and tried again. And found the call wouldn't go through.

"Great. She must have thought this was a spam number and blocked it."

Which meant she wouldn't listen to the message, either. Someday soon, she'd have a long conversation with her sister regarding her privacy fears.

The clock had just past two in the afternoon when the chief called again. Vanessa went into the other room while Carter talked to his boss. A few minutes later, he came to find her.

"Listen, the chief wants to talk with us at the station. But first, your car is drivable. It's been processed, and he got the door so it will open. We can pick it up. After the holidays, you can take it in to get any of the cosmetic damage dealt with. The department will pay for it."

"Really? That's fantastic!"

If she had her car, she could go get some clothes and necessities to get her through the next few days.

"Why don't we head out? I'll drop you off to get your car."

She agreed immediately.

"Great. Can you grab a couple of bottled waters from the fridge? I need to pack up my computer."

"Sure."

Within ten minutes, he'd locked up his house and escorted her to his vehicle. "You know, we should grab your prescription on the way to get your car. That way, we won't need to backtrack."

"You're driving. If you don't mind stopping, I'm good with it."

At the pharmacy, they went through the drive-through and collected her meds. She popped a capsule into her mouth and washed it down with water. Then they were on the way to get her car. The closer they drove to the impound lot, the more tense her muscles became.

"Vanessa, what's wrong?"

Of course, he'd noticed.

"Nothing. I'm being silly." When he waited, she huffed an annoyed sigh. "Really. I'm embarrassed, but I just can't help feeling something will happen."

"Considering everything, I'd say a little paranoia is reasonable."

"You're the only person I know who can use *paranoia* and *reasonable* in the same sentence without being insulting."

He chuckled, a deep, warm laugh that made her smile.

"It's all good." He parked along the street. "We walk from here."

He led her through a gate and scanned the parking lot. "There's your Jeep."

He pointed to a space in the middle of the lot.

She saw her poor crumpled car. "It still looks kind of sad."

"The important thing is it is drivable. You can worry about how it looks later."

She shrugged. He had a point. She went in, signed the paperwork and collected her keys. Warren, the man behind the desk, nodded at her thanks.

"Here's the ticket to get you out of the lot." He handed her a ticket with a scan code on one side. "Drive careful, now, miss. Always lock your doors."

He reminded her so much of her father, all big and brusque on the outside but soft as a marshmallow on the inside. Longing for one of her father's bear hugs swamped her. Her throat ached with unshed tears. She blinked them back.

Carter was waiting at the door. Vanessa regained her composure. "I'll be careful."

She walked out of the building and walked down the two steps to the sidewalk to Carter's side.

"Now that you have your Jeep," he said as he began walking toward the parking lot, "I'll follow you there."

Vanessa planted her feet so fast, she swayed forward.

Carter walked two steps before he seemed to realize he was walking alone. He pivoted to face her.

"Is something the matter?"

"No. I guess not. I just got nervous about being alone." She hated the quiver in her voice but was powerless to stop the fear coursing through her.

He moved to her side. "You won't be alone. I'm going to get in my car, then I'll be right behind you. Although, if you don't mind, I might leave you at the station for an hour to go check on my mom. But only if the opportunity presents itself."

She shooed him away. "Go. Get your car. I'll wait until you're behind me to pull out on the street. I'll be fine."

To prove to him that she meant what she said, she moved toward her car, shivering when she looked back and saw him moving in the opposite direction.

She could do this. She was a strong, independent woman. And, like he said, it was the middle of the day. Who'd be bold enough to attack someone on a sunny day in the impound lot?

Reaching her Jeep, she used her fob to unlock the door. She raised her head and saw movement reflected in the glass. Her eyes shot to the movement.

A man was racing toward her.

Whirling around, she fell back against the door. Her arms shot out protectively. The man slammed against her, knocking the breath from her body. She struggled against him. His fingers dug into her upper arms. He yanked at her, trying to pull her away from her Jeep. She dug in her heels and rammed her elbow into his throat. When his hold loosened, she wrenched herself away from him and screamed.

"Carter!" Her heart pounded so hard, her chest hurt.

Her attacker lunged toward her again. His fist hit her injured shoulder. She yelped when pain shot through her body.

Would she live through the day?

SEVEN

"Carter!"

He whipped around at her terrified shriek. He couldn't see her, but Vanessa was in trouble. Checking his weapon, Carter took off at a run, making it back to where he left her in a third of the time it took him to reach his cruiser. After slipping through the gate, he took another two steps.

His heart nearly stopped. Vanessa and an assailant were wrestling at her car. The door of her Jeep was open. The young man shoved her toward the opening. Vanessa was strong and fit, but her attacker had bulk in his favor.

A gun was lying on the ground between them.

Carter hadn't wanted to leave Vanessa outside the impound office. But he thought nothing would happen to her between the building and her car.

Her well-being had become far more important to him than that of a regular case he worked. In the very brief time they'd been acquainted, he'd grown attached to her. The rare sound of her laugh felt like home.

He had rejected the thought as ridiculous the moment it went through his head. He was a seasoned police lieutenant with the Sterling Ridge Police Department. Before that, he'd walked the homicide beat in a big city until his mother had needed him full-time. He wasn't someone who allowed his emotions to rule his decisions.

He thought he needed to be strictly professional in their dealings. Limit their close proximity. Keep their discussions focused on the job.

Now, she was in danger...again.

"Police! Put your hands up!" Carter held his Glock steady. He couldn't shoot. Not without risking Vanessa's life. Even a leg shot would be risky with all the twisting the pair was doing.

With a wrenching move, the assailant spun, using Vanessa as a shield, his arm tight across her throat. Vanessa choked. She clawed at the arm that was constricting her breathing, her face growing red.

"Come on, man. You don't want to hurt her." Carter tried to coax the assailant back from the violence vibrating in the air. After so many attacks and one murder, however, he doubted the man holding on to her even cared.

Behind the Jeep, Carter watched the door of the impound office open slowly until the space was large enough for person to slip out sideways. A familiar figure eased through the gap. Lieutenant Ryan Douglass inched his way down the two steps and came toward them, his weapon raised and ready.

Calm descended over Carter like a cloak. He had backup. When he'd informed the chief that he and Vanessa were heading here, his boss must have sent Ryan, just in case. The assailant didn't have another gun, that he could see. He aimed a focused look at his opponent. The young man had both hands full. Vanessa wasn't giving him time to reach for another weapon, even if he had one. She twisted and churned, her hands pulling at his arm, and her feet stomped and kicked. Even while Carter watched, her left heel slammed against the man's shin, making him grunt in pain.

Carter risked a glance at Vanessa's face. Rather than fear, fury blazed from her expression, as her pretty mouth curled into a snarl.

"I'll kill her! Don't come any closer or she's going to die!" the man yelled.

Vanessa stilled at the man's words.

The arm pinned across her neck relaxed slightly. The attacker flexed his fingers.

That was his mistake. Vanessa half turned and grabbed his arm, yanking it up toward her face.

Carter knew what she'd do a second before she did it. Jerking her hands apart to bare his wrist, Vanessa sank her teeth into the tender skin.

Yelling, her attacker hurled her from him.

The moment she left his arms, the attacker seemed to realize his mistake. He dove for the gun on the ground. Carter kicked it away with one smooth swipe. Ryan rounded the Jeep, trapping him between them.

"Vanessa," Carter said. "Please go inside the office and wait with Warren."

She gave her would-be kidnapper one final look filled with loathing before complying.

"Carter? That's not the man I heard on the phone."

He nodded. He'd already figured that out by her expression when she heard the young man's voice.

The question remained—if this man wasn't the ringleader, then how did he fit into this puzzle?

Carter needed to get some answers, and fast. Because the fact that the killer had someone waiting here for Vanessa told him several things, each one more disturbing than the last.

First, the killer's desperation had escalated. How many people did he have working for him and what hold did he have on them?

Second, how did he know they were coming to the impound lot? The idea that his house or phone had been compromised or bugged was doubtful. Until the fire, he'd had no intention of bringing her to his home. Also, the decision to come get her Jeep hadn't been made until the phone call this morning.

He could only think of one thing. There was a leak, somewhere. Somehow, private information had made its way into a killer's hands.

Someone at the police department itself might be the leak. The thought of dealing with a dirty cop shook him. He had a few people he would trust with his own life. Chief Melody Kaiser lived and breathed justice. There was no way she'd betray him.

Lieutenant Brett Talbot was more than a partner. He was also Carter's best friend. They'd been on the Sterling Ridge wrestling team together from first grade all the way up through their senior varsity year. They even went to the state wrestling championship tournament together. When Carter left to seek his career elsewhere, they'd kept in touch and met up when they could. Upon his return, he'd found his relationship with his friend had survived all the upheavals of both their lives.

Again, Brett was someone that Carter believed one hundred percent would have his back.

Even Lieutenant Ryan Douglass had earned his trust during his short duration at this job.

He glanced back to the office and watched Vanessa enter and vanish from sight. And a single truth stood out. He'd trust them with his life.

But not with hers.

Vanessa rushed into the office, her legs shaking so hard, she collapsed into the chair along the wall. It wasn't the attack that made her feel so weak. Yes, she'd been terrified at the confrontation, and when her assailant grabbed her around the throat, she'd thought she'd die. But the moment she saw Carter, she had felt safe.

No, it was hearing the youthful tenor voice speaking so close to her ear. Not because she recognized it. But because she didn't. The voice she'd heard speaking to Mandy had been deeper, slower. It had definitely been disguised, but there was no doubt that the man outside had not been the one Mandy had called.

How many people were involved in this illegal business? Mandy's dead eyes floated before her. She shuddered. Both Mandy and the kid out there today were young—too young to throw their lives away like this.

But they had. Anger surged inside her. She wanted to know who did this. He needed to pay for destroying so many lives. Not just the babies themselves. Hopefully these children were finding homes that loved them, even if they were kidnapped. No, this whole operation ruthlessly destroyed families for money.

Her dad had always told her not to become too enamored of money. The treasures on earth could be used for good or for evil, depending on one's attitude. She'd always thought him overstating the problem with greed.

Now, she knew better and had a new respect for her father.

Warren stood up from his desk and painfully made his way to the counter. "I'm sorry, miss. I called nine-one-one as soon as I saw that punk approach you. If I were younger, I would have come to your aid myself!"

For the first time, she noticed the walker next to his chair. She smiled at his remorse-filled face.

"I understand. Carter—I mean Lieutenant Flint—was close.

He heard me and came running. But I think your emergency call saved my life."

She wasn't placating the older man. She'd seen the dread and frustration warring in Carter's eyes. He wanted to end the threat against her. Shooting the kid remained impossible while she was in his way. Having the other cop show up had changed the power balance and given them the edge.

She'd bitten that foul man's arm. Remembering, she gagged.

"You okay, miss?"

"I bit that man," she gasped, trying to ignore the taste he'd left in her mouth. Like motor oil. She gagged again.

He chuckled. "You have grit. I have something that might help."

After pulling open a drawer, he held up a bag of portable, single-serving mouthwash packets. She saw the fresh-mint label and gratefully accepted one.

"I'll be right back." She stepped into the bathroom. A minute later, the urge to vomit had faded. Her mouth now tasted like cool mint. She'd gladly take the side effect of the slight burning sensation over the aftertaste left from biting the villain. When she returned to the office, Carter's presence filled the room.

Her pulse kicked up a notch. She took a deep breath then pasted a smile on her face as she greeted him.

"Did he hurt you?" Carter asked, brushing off her greeting. His eyes zeroed in on her throat. Reflexively, she rubbed the tender area.

"I'm fine. Although I think his coat gave me rugburn on my neck." She wasn't kidding. It still stung.

In two steps, he'd invaded her space and had gently removed her hand. "Hmm. He did. Unfortunately, there's not much we can do about that."

She nodded. She needed to talk with him, but didn't want

to discuss her suspicions in front of Warren. The man had been sweet and protective, but he wasn't law enforcement.

The bottom line was that she didn't want another to be put in jeopardy because of her.

"Thanks for your help, Warren. We'll get out of your hair."

Carter motioned for her to follow him. She waited until they were once again outside, then asked him about her attacker.

"He's on his way to the station with Lieutenant Douglass. Let's get your Jeep, then I'll follow you to the police station."

She grimaced. "I'm sorry. I know you wanted to go see your mom."

In an instant, he'd rounded until he stood in front of her, halting her progress. His warm hand touched her chin, nudging her gaze to meet his. Warmth spread from where he touched. She probably looked like a tomato with her red hair and hot cheeks.

"You have nothing to apologize for." His eyebrows lowered. "You're the victim. I shouldn't have left you alone like I did."

That didn't sit well. "We can pass the blame, but the reality is that I'm an adult and you shouldn't have to babysit me."

He shrugged and dropped her chin. "It's my job."

His casual response stung. Vanessa fumed. She was a duty? She stomped along beside him, then got into her Jeep without another word.

"I'll follow you," he reiterated.

She nodded.

Carter hesitated. "Vanessa. I didn't mean that the way it sounded."

"What? This is your job. I'm not hurt. You are an officer and I am being stalked by a killer. I get it. The sooner we find this creep, the sooner I can go back to my life."

Temper colored her words, but she didn't care. The past twenty-four hours had pushed her beyond what she could endure and remain polite.

"It's just—"

"Carter, it's fine." She took pleasure in biting off the word. Tanner always said when Vanessa said something was fine, he knew it was time to duck and run for cover.

"Whatever." Carter waited until she was in the car, buckled up and the vehicle was locked before he stalked back to his cruiser.

Part of her felt bad for pushing him away so ruthlessly. But his statement had reminded her that no matter how handsome and good a man was, she wasn't interested. Never again would she allow a man into her heart.

It was a bitter acknowledgement, but she had no other option. The one time she'd allowed herself to fall in love, Nolan had taken everything from her. She wouldn't give a man that kind of power over her ever again.

She pulled onto the street, aware of Carter's cruiser two car lengths behind her. A single tear tracked down her cheek.

EIGHT

What had just happened?

Carter knew the moment he'd said he was only doing his job that he'd made a colossal mistake. He puffed out his cheeks and blew the air out in a hard whoosh. It had been so long since he'd had another woman to worry about besides his mother.

Vanessa had a bit of a temper. She was also smart, compassionate and so beautiful it made his heart ache with longing just to stand close to her. Never in his life, even before he'd decided he was not good husband material, had he felt so instantly and consistently drawn to a woman.

It made him want things he knew he couldn't have.

She'd be better off with someone else. Surely, in a family as large as hers, there was someone she could stay with and still help the police find other possible pregnant targets.

His mind shifted to the young man on his way to be booked. They already knew that the killer used people who had some kind of serious issue, like debt. If they looked into that area, maybe they could pinpoint those vulnerable. It was a long shot, but anything they could do to prevent a kidnapping would be a good place to start.

Ahead of him, Vanessa's Jeep purred into the police-station parking lot. She backed into a space between two SUVs, her vehicle smoothly centered between the yellow lines. Some of his colleagues couldn't back into a space that well.

He whistled. She continued to impress him.

He parked his cruiser in its designated space. He'd leave the cruiser for Brett to use and take his own truck when he left.

Meeting Vanessa at the door, he opened it for her and waved for her to walk in front of him.

"Chivalry?" She raised one eyebrow, apparently having forgiven him on the short drive.

He shook his head. He didn't want to give a cold answer, but she needed to be fully aware of the risks. "Not completely. While I try to be a gentleman, in this case, I also want to make sure anyone shooting for you has to go through me first."

She shivered, her eyes widening. "Thanks. I hope no one does."

He led her to the chief's office without commenting. At this point, they both knew that his presence wouldn't stop the killer, or his minions, from coming for her with the intent to kill.

She wasn't safe as long as she was in town.

Chief Kaiser looked up when he knocked on the frame of her open office door. She liked her officers to feel they were welcome to stop in whenever they had an issue or a question. When her door was closed, they all knew only to disturb her in an emergency situation.

"Lieutenant. Nurse Hall. Please, come in. And close the door behind you." Chief Kaiser rose from her seat and gestured to the two chairs facing her desk. She waited until her visitors sat before sinking into her sturdy chair once more. "Lieutenant Douglass brought in the man who attacked you today."

Carter tapped his foot against the floor. "What do we know about him?"

She glanced at her notes. "He's twenty-two and has a drug addiction. He sometimes takes jobs for drug money. Apparently, he has quite the clientele. Mostly petty crimes. This was his first hit job, or at least he claims it was."

Vanessa leaned forward. "Did he say who hired him?"

Chief Kaiser sighed. "If only it were that easy. No, he has a website. I have our tech guys on it. It's an innocent enough looking site. But people contact him to purchase 'products.' Then he calls them to discuss delivery details."

Carter couldn't hold in a groan. "Let me guess. His phone is a burner."

"Yes, it is."

"So we've not learned anything," Vanessa said, discouraged.

"Not quite." Carter informed them of his thoughts about how the killer hired people to do his dirty work. "We know that Mandy had massive debt and was a compulsive shopper. This guy is feeding a drug addiction. The janitor who kidnapped the first baby had a gambling addiction. He lures those who are in desperate situations."

The chief blinked at him. "Most of the people he's hired, that we know of, have been somehow connected with hospitals or with clinics. We can start interviewing the local hospital staff, but that will be an overwhelming task. We're a small department."

He sank back against his seat, suddenly exhausted. "Plus, he generally doesn't get people from the same area twice in a row."

Vanessa shifted in her seat. "Maybe. But we know he's on crunch time here. He needs a baby now. So I'm guessing his options might be limited."

"True. You said you recognized his voice?" The chief raised her eyebrows at Vanessa and waited.

"I think so. But it wasn't a voice I could place immediately, so I'm guessing it's not someone I see on a regular basis. And if it's someone who has access to a wide range of hospitals, it could be someone who delivers medical supplies or works on our equipment. The list of possibilities is huge."

"The way I see it, we have to protect you. And we have to prevent another newborn abduction. Ideas?"

Carter opened his mouth, but Vanessa beat him to it.

"I told Carter that I could help try and locate the Amish women in the local communities whose due date is imminent."

The chief smiled for the first time. "I like that idea. It would help us keep you close. Why are you shaking your head, Lieutenant?"

Both women turned to stare at him.

"Is it wise? Yes, we could use Vanessa's knowledge. But keeping her nearby? Chief, someone obviously knows her well enough that she's in danger. And..." He lowered his voice. "I'm concerned that there may be a leak in our department."

"Surely not!" the chief blurted.

Vanessa's mouth dropped open.

"Think about it. How else did this guy," he paused for a moment, "I'm just gonna call him the Baby Thief for now. Anyway, how did the Baby Thief know that Vanessa would be at the impound this morning? Clearly, he had information that only we should have known."

"The Baby Thief?" the chief echoed. "I suppose it was only a matter of time before he acquired a name. I don't like where your mind is heading. But I agree, unfortunately."

The chief drummed her fingertips on her desk. "Our resources are already stretched to the limit. I have increased our security efforts at both the hospital and the clinic. This case is the number-one priority right now and all shifts have assignments they are investigating."

"What do I do?" Vanessa whispered. "I have nowhere to go. I refuse to put my sister and her son or my sister-in-law in danger. There is no one else for at least three more days. By that time, Tanner and Zach will be back with their families, and my parents will be home from their cruise."

"We'll have to keep you safe for three more days."

He was pretty sure they all heard the unspoken question of how they'd do that.

Carter thought about his schedule. The department operated on a four-day-on, three-day-off schedule. Today was day four for him. An idea surfaced. One that conflicted with his desire to distance himself. But if anything happened to Vanessa— His entire soul rebelled at the mere idea.

He was going to regret this.

"I need to go rogue for a while." Carter dragged out the words, not really wanting to say them, but feeling it was the best option. "I know I'm supposed to be off for the next three days. Obviously, that can't happen. But no one else needs to know that. I will keep Vanessa with me. We will work together to form a list of possible targets. But I can't go to my home. Because I think my place is probably even now being watched."

He knew the chief would agree. He wanted her to because he needed to protect Vanessa. He'd failed his sister. He wouldn't make that mistake again.

Could he keep her alive and not become emotionally compromised?

Vanessa felt like the breath had been knocked out of her.

Someone wanted her dead. To the point where Carter was appointing himself her 24/7 bodyguard.

"But, Carter, what about your mom?" She held her hand out like a school crossing guard. "I am grateful for all your help, but I can't disrupt your family that way."

"You're not."

She gave him a disbelieving look.

"Vanessa, I'm serious. My mom is with her cousin. She's safe. I'd already cleared it with Alice for a few days. We have an arrangement where she has a room at her house for my mom whenever I need a few days. Trust me. This has happened before, and it will again. It's not a big deal."

The chief interrupted before she could protest. "Nurse Hall, the lieutenant is correct. Plus, you are our best advantage in finding the Baby Thief's targets. We need your help. Unofficially, of course."

Vanessa gave in. She couldn't deny the chief, not when the woman was asking for her help in saving babies.

She'd always try to protect mothers and their children. To say no would go against her core beliefs.

"It would look odd if you didn't complete your shift," the chief said to Carter. "I will not announce that you are still working. As far as anyone else knows, you are off the clock starting the end of shift today. What about Brett?"

"Let's not tell him anything. I trust him, but he's a horrible liar."

Not a bad trait in a friend. Vanessa's thoughts immediately flew to Nolan, who lied with the ease of taking a clean breath.

A few moments later, she and Carter were dismissed. They met up with Brett as they were coming from the station.

"Hey, Carter."

"Brett. Good day, eh?" Brett's face went still, then he nodded.

How would Carter explain her presence?

A few minutes later, it became obvious that Carter had no intention of explaining.

And equally obvious that Brett wouldn't ask.

Burning with curiosity, she waited until they were sitting in his pickup truck. "Why didn't he ask you why I was with you?"

Carter sent her a grin. She flushed in response.

"We have a code. When one of us says 'Good day, eh?' the other knows not to ask questions. Most likely, Brett thinks I'm on a mission for the chief, but once I'm off shift, it will never occur to him that I'm still working because we left the cruiser behind."

She didn't understand why a secret code was necessary and said so.

He hesitated. "Brett and I have known each other forever. Since we were about five. I grew up in a great home. It was Mom and Dad, and later, my kid sister, Gretta. Brett grew up in chaos. There were times when he needed a place to crash but couldn't tell me why. We developed the code so he could tell me he needed space. Later, after my sister died, I began to use the code, too."

She sucked in a breath. She hadn't known that his only sibling had died. Should she ask? Not ask?

"I don't know what to do with that information," she finally said. "If you want to tell me more, I'll listen. But I don't want to be intrusive."

Carter ran a hand through his military-short dark brown hair. A muscle in his jaw worked. She let him stew, knowing he'd either tell her or he wouldn't. She'd respect his choice either way.

"I don't talk about it," he finally said.

"I understand."

He shot her a look. "You do, don't you? For someone with such a feisty temperament, you're an excellent listener."

He thought she was feisty? Was that good or bad? It sounded like a compliment in his deep tones, but she wasn't sure.

"Umm, thanks?"

Carter chuckled. "Feisty is good. It means you don't let people walk over you."

Her heart darkened. "Not anymore. I used to. Then I learned to stand up for myself."

"My sister never got that chance. She'd been bullied online by a group of girls from school. One of them had been her best friend. Gretta made the mistake of catching the attention of the boy the other girl liked. When she went out on a date with him, the 'mean girls,' as I call them, decided to make her life miserable. A week before her sixteenth birthday, she overdosed. We called nine-one-one, but it was too late."

Vanessa was sick to her stomach. "That's awful! How did you find out who bullied her?"

"It was all in private messages on her laptop. Including messages in an app from school. The other girls were all expelled. The school had a zero-tolerance policy. It was too little, too late."

She thought he was done. That he'd said the worst of it. She was mistaken.

"My mom blames me for her death."

Her blood froze. "What? How on earth is it your fault?"

"I was the man of the house. Have been since my dad passed away. I should have noticed."

That was wrong on so many levels.

"I don't buy that. She didn't notice, and she's the mother. It's not your fault. The girls who tormented your sister are to blame. Not you."

"I know it. And on good days, she does, too. However, those days are few and far between."

Vanessa clenched her hands. With all that Carter had suffered, he was still willing to go out of his way for a stranger, such as her.

She hadn't done that. She'd discreetly pushed her family away to guard her darkest secret and her pain. Shame spilled inside her gut. She had a large, boisterous family that loved her and she had not treasured them for the gift they were.

Was it too late?

She turned her face to stare out the window, pondering what she'd heard, struggling to process her own emotions. The radio on Carter's shoulder beeped.

They both fell silent as they listened to the dispatcher announce a structure fire with injuries. She grimaced. It sounded like a bad one.

"An apartment fire—that's not good," Carter said, echoing her thoughts.

"Yeah. Did they just say they needed four ambulances?"

He turned up the volume of his personal shoulder radio. They both listened as Dispatch repeated the call, clarifying details. The chatter that followed confirmed that emergency vehicles were en route.

"It's going to take them a bit," Carter mused. "That's almost to the other side of the city."

"Will they call in help from other departments?"

"They're going to have to. Sterling Ridge can't handle that alone."

For the second time in as many days, the urge to say a prayer nudged at her. If it had been a prayer for herself, Vanessa most likely would have ignored the impulse. However, this was for others. People who may not have turned their back on God, as she had. While she may not deserve His mercy, surely they did.

Quietly, she whispered a short prayer.

"Amen," Carter echoed when she finished.

Apparently, she hadn't been as quiet as she'd thought. Strangely, that didn't disturb her as much as it would have a few days ago. Of course, it was only Carter. And she trusted him.

The fact that she trusted him so completely bothered her. When had he gotten through her defenses?

The radio on Carter's shoulder beeped again. For a second, she thought they were calling in additional departments to help with the structure fire.

Darlene's voice echoed through the close space of the truck cab. "Crime in progress. Attempted abduction at Miller's Marketplace and Produce."

That was an Amish-run grocery store. They sold mostly home grown and homemade food there.

The next details chilled her. "Victim escaped abductor. Witness says suspect has fled the scene. Ambulance is to stage at the Amish church a half mile from the scene until police arrive on scene and declare it's safe. The victim is a twenty-one-year-old female. She's in labor."

Vanessa froze. If the victim was going into labor and at an Amish store, she was almost certainly the next potential victim. And there were no more ambulances available in the local area. They had all been sent to the fire.

She and Carter needed to go to the Amish store, now.

NINE

Vanessa half spun in her seat toward Carter. She reached out and grabbed his hand. He shot her a surprised look. She yanked her hand back as if she'd received an electric shock. Her cheeks burned, but she couldn't let a little embarrassment hinder her.

"Carter, they don't have any ambulances to spare. They're all headed to the fire. This woman…"

He'd turned a corner and was in the process of making a U-turn. "Put that light on my dashboard, right against the window."

He pointed to a portable police light. She positioned it and flipped it on. Her stomach clenched. She forced herself to take a deep breath. She couldn't afford to panic. A patient needed her. Two patients, including the unborn child.

Would they make it in time? Thoughts and worries bombarded her.

"What if he comes back for her? If she's in labor, she'll have no chance of fighting him off."

And the Amish were by nature absolute pacifists. They wouldn't use a weapon to protect her. Would they fight at all? She didn't know enough about their culture to answer that question.

Carter didn't answer her query. He hit the call switch on

his truck phone and spat out a phone number. Brett's name appeared on the dashboard. For a moment, she wondered why he didn't just say Brett's name. Surely, his best friend was on speed dial. Then she dismissed it as unimportant. The phone rang once. Then again.

"Come on, buddy. Pick up the phone." Carter's fingers drummed on the steering wheel.

"Hey, Carter. What do you need?" Brett said.

"Did you hear the call over at Miller's?"

"On my way there."

"Good. I need to stage at the church. Call me when the scene is secure."

She waited for Brett to ask why Carter couldn't come directly to the scene. Then recalled he'd seen her with Carter and would put two and two together that a midwife was coming to the scene. Didn't that go against their plan? She worried her bottom lip. There was so much potential for tragedy here.

Carter hung up the phone without another word. She blinked. It usually took her five minutes to get off the phone with Darlene or Lillian. Ten with her mother. Men communicated differently.

"I thought we were going to try and 'go rogue.'" She made air quotes when she said the last two words.

He smirked, throwing her a wink. "We are. I called Brett's personal phone. Not his work phone."

"Was that why you said the number and not his name?"

"It is. Plus, being a guy, his contact name in my phone list, while not rude or vulgar, is rather tongue-in-cheek and a joke from years ago. Probably not something he'd want you to hear."

She snorted. "I get it. My name in Tanner's phone is 'my sissy with a temper.' I don't have a temper."

He coughed. She narrowed her eyes. "Did you just laugh? Sorry. Not important. You trust Brett, obviously."

"I do. He's not going to tell anyone that you and I are together. But I didn't want anything on his work phone. If he saw my call coming in on his personal number, I knew he'd take it where no one else could hear it."

Carter really was worried about a mole in the department.

"Turn left, there." She pointed to the next dirt road. "I know a shortcut."

She half expected him to ignore her suggestion. She'd worked with far too many men that had discounted her advice because she was a woman, pretty—or so she'd been told—and a nurse...not a doctor.

A thrill of pleasure tingled in her heart when he turned without hesitation.

"I'm not familiar with this route, so you'll have to tell me where to go."

She directed him through a series of twists and turns. At one point, they went over a rickety bridge that resembled a raft. He ignored the GPS that continued to recalibrate and tried to return them to the main road. He didn't even balk when she instructed him to ignore a detour sign. When the sign announcing the church came into view, he grinned at her.

"You can be my navigator anytime, Vanessa Hall. You shaved five minutes off this trip. I wonder why the GPS didn't reroute to the back roads."

"That raftlike bridge washed out during a storm last year. It wasn't on the list of urgent repairs, so it never got repaired. The local community wanted that bridge so they wouldn't have to constantly route their buggies out of the way to go about their business. So they got together and fixed it. One of the families owns a lumberyard. They made it work, but it's never been updated in the system. As far as the state is concerned, that bridge is still out. Only locals use it."

They waited in the parking lot for nearly ten minutes before Brett called. Carter accepted the call, not even trying to divert it back to his phone for privacy. Brett's gravelly voice boomed through the speakers.

"The scene is all clear. The suspect has fled the area."

"Is he armed?" Carter asked.

"No one here noticed any weapons." There was a pause. They could hear voices in the background. "The girl behind the counter said he ran when others appeared on the scene. Seemed spooked to see so many people."

Carter frowned. "How many others are on the scene?"

"Five," Brett replied. "Including the woman he tried to kidnap."

"Okay. I'm heading to your location now." Carter disconnected the call and aimed the truck toward the store. It took them less than three minutes to arrive.

He braked outside the store and shut off the engine. "I'm assuming you'll take control of the woman in labor? While you work with her, I'm going to see if I can get a description of the abductor."

She nodded, her mind already on the woman waiting inside. She had to be terrified. She opened her door.

Carter touched her hand, halting her. She looked at him, surprised by the soft smile lifting his lips. "You were amazing, by the way."

She sat for a second, stunned. "Thanks. We make a good team."

She left the vehicle and headed inside. They did make a good team, Carter and her.

She shoved all irrelevant thoughts aside and approached the young woman who was standing behind the counter, wringing her hands. A quick glance assured her this was not the expectant mother.

"Good afternoon," she greeted in her most reassuring manner. "I'm Nurse Vanessa Hall, a certified nurse midwife with the Sterling Ridge Medical Clinic."

Relief flooded the young woman's face. Her shoulders drooped. *"Danke.* I'll take you back."

Vanessa followed her to the rear of the store. She caught Carter's gaze and pointed to the back room. He dipped his chin in acknowledgment. Then she forgot about him.

The expecting woman was in the back storage room with an older woman. Judging by the similarities in their features, she guessed the other woman was either her mother or her aunt.

"Hi. I'm Vanessa. I'm a midwife."

"Abigail," she gasped through a contraction.

"Okay, Abigail, let's get you as comfortable as possible and I'll ask you some questions."

"I'm Abigail's mother. My sister is over there." The older woman gestured to another woman standing near the wall.

"How can we help?" The aunt asked.

Within five minutes, Vanessa had the situation under control. "Is this your first baby?"

"Jah," the woman panted, blushing.

"You're doing fine, Abigail. I'll help you through this."

Vanessa bit back her smile. She needed to remain professional. By the time the paramedics arrived, it was too late to move the suffering woman to the ambulance. Vanessa nodded to them. She'd worked with both Sydney and Nathan before.

She gave them a concise report of the patient's status. When Nathan tried to assume control, Abigail began to panic.

Vanessa turned to him. "Nathan, you will assist me, but I am the midwife she is comfortable with. She can't be moved to the hospital. We are delivering this baby here."

He retreated.

Two hours later, Abigail cradled her son in her arms.

Vanessa gave her some encouraging words, then stepped aside and let the paramedics check both Abigail and her child. Although they looked well, it never hurt to check.

Nathan started talking about transporting them to the hospital. Abigail bluntly refused. "Why? My *boppli* is here, *jah*? He's healthy. I don't need to go to the hospital."

Nathan flushed.

"You were planning on a home birth, anyway, right?" Vanessa asked.

"Jah." She nodded and gave Nathan a level stare.

For all her shy manners, Abigail had a backbone when it counted.

"Are you refusing care?" Nathan asked for confirmation, confused.

"You've already cared for me. I want to go home now."

Vanessa pressed her lips together so the smile wouldn't sneak onto her face. Soon, however, watching Abigail with her newborn stirred other emotions. Tears stung her eyes.

She hadn't been this weepy in years. Yet in the past two days, she felt like she never stopped crying. Too many memories filled her mind.

She glanced at Abigail and her new son. The woman and child were safe, for now. But what would happen when the ringleader learned of this new baby? Would the baby be targeted?

Steel entered her heart. Somehow, they had to protect both this mother and her child.

Carter completed his conference with Brett just as the pregnant mother's aunt entered the room and told them that her niece had given birth to a son. Excusing himself, he made his way to the back room and knocked discreetly on the door.

Sydney, one of the paramedics, cracked the door open about an inch and peered through the gap. When she saw him standing there, she swung the door open the rest of the way and gestured for him to enter, placing a finger at her lips.

"Shhh. We don't want to disturb them."

Carter nodded, fighting back a spurt of irritation. Like he couldn't have figured that out for himself.

He stopped just inside the door. Carter's gaze was drawn to Vanessa and he couldn't look away. She was cleaning up the infant, who fussed and whined, but wasn't crying. Still, he had to grin that Sydney had shushed him when the baby himself was creating such a racket. He watched as the red-haired midwife efficiently wrapped the child in blankets provided by an older Amish woman. Then she murmured her thanks before settling the newborn in his mother's outstretched arms.

What immediately struck Carter was the expression on her face. It was a mixture of sorrow and joy, two emotions he'd never seen play out together so seamlessly before. What was going through her mind?

Then fear, anger and determination took over. Vanessa stood abruptly, her slender hands clenching into fists at her side.

Carter knew immediately where her mind had gone.

Moving quietly, he crossed the space between them and planted himself next to her. So close, their shoulders brushed. She stiffened, then relaxed.

"Vanessa," he whispered.

She didn't speak, just looked up at him with deep eyes.

"We will protect them. I know she's a target. I've asked her uncle to locate her husband and bring him here. I will personally ensure that she is guarded until they are removed from danger."

Vanessa closed her eyes and breathed in so deeply, her shoulders rose and fell with her exhale. When she looked at him, the trust in her blue gaze hit him like a punch to the gut. A yearning so strong filled him, he instinctively stepped away from her, then regretted it when hurt filled her face before her expression went blank. Desperate to fix his mistake, he grabbed her hand without thinking, then stopped, unsure what to say.

She glanced at their joined fingers. She squeezed, then released him. This time, she was the one who put distance between them.

A noise behind them reminded him they weren't alone in the room. He ignored Sydney and Nathan.

"I'll go and watch for her husband." He looked at the new mother. "You stay with her?"

"Absolutely."

Satisfied, he strode out of the room, fighting the urge to run. Brett gave him a concerned look, but he wasn't ready to talk about his feelings, not even with his best friend.

Shrugging, Brett went to walk around the perimeter again. "Just in case this guy decides to return."

The bell above the entrance jingled. Carter spun. An Amish man with a short beard stepped inside. He knew Amish men didn't start growing a beard until they married. He couldn't have been more than twenty-five. Probably not even that.

The man saw Carter and caution overtook his every movement. He crossed his arms across his chest. "I'm Henry Lantz. I'm here to see my wife, Abigail."

Carter flashed him a smile, hoping to reassure the young husband. "Of course. I'm Lieutenant Carter Flint. Your wife is in the back with the paramedics and a certified nurse midwife."

The young man's shoulders loosened. His arms dropped to his side. "*Danke*. Is she *gut*?"

"I believe so, yes. Why don't we go and see her now?"

He let the concerned husband walk in front of him. When the door opened, a soft female voice cried out. "Henry! Look...we have a *sohn*."

Carter allowed the little family to have a few moments together with their newest member before approaching them. He quietly asked Sydney and Nathan to give him some time with the Lantz family. Nathan looked ready to argue, but Sydney grabbed the other paramedic by the arm and all but dragged him out.

"I'm afraid I have to speak with you about what happened before the child came."

Abigail paled. "The man who tried to take me?"

Carter nodded. "Yes."

Henry positioned himself protectively near his family, his arm around his wife. "Have you caught him?"

"We have not. But we know why he attacked you, Mrs. Lantz." Carter lowered himself onto a chair. Standing over people tended to intimidate them, and that was the opposite of what he wanted. "We have learned there is an illegal adoption ring—"

"What is that?" Henry interrupted.

Carter rubbed his chin. It was a very grim story, but he tried to be gentle in his report. "There is a group of people who are stealing newborns and trying to sell them to new families. Right now, it's unclear if the adoptive families are aware of the fact that the babies they get are kidnapped."

"How do you know this is why he came after me?" Abigail asked. "It could be a coincidence, *jah*?"

He wished he could agree with her, just to give her some peace. Because if he said yes, it wouldn't be long before they had to accept their little one wasn't out of danger. Not yet.

"I'm sorry, ma'am. This particular ring has been targeting Amish communities."

By now, tears flowed down her cheeks. Abigail buried her face in her husband's shoulder. She cradled her sleeping son close. Henry dropped a soft kiss on Abigail's *kapp*.

"I will take my wife and *boppli* to visit family in Ohio," he announced.

Carter gave him an approving nod. "Will you accept a police escort?"

The parents agreed to that. Carter impressed upon the others in the room the importance of keeping the family's whereabouts a secret. Ohio wasn't that far away. For a kidnapper desperate to obtain a newborn, that distance wouldn't pose an insurmountable challenge.

He'd see if Brett would go with them. It was only a couple of hours away. He didn't want anyone else aware of it. Since the family had refused to go to the hospital, they could keep the number of people aware of the birth—and where they were disappearing to—down to a minimum.

After Brett had come into the room and learned about the plan, it was easy enough to get the family bundled up and prepped for the journey. Brett made a quick jog to the local big-box store for a car seat and other baby necessities. Abigail's mother couldn't go with her, but her next younger sister was unmarried, so she would go along to help her sister with anything.

"Since they'll be visiting family in Sutter Springs, Ohio, I'll stop in and visit Chief Mike Spencer at the Sutter Springs Police Department," Brett said. "I'll update him on the case and explain we're keeping things on the down-low. The precinct there needs to know that Abigail's baby was a target so they can keep an eye on the situation. Am I wrong?"

Carter sighed. He should have known Brett would figure things out. The man was nearly a genius, and that was no joke.

"Don't say anything." Brett patted his shoulder. "What you don't say, I can't repeat."

"Understood."

Carter watched Brett pull out of the drive with his cruiser full to capacity with the Amish family. Vanessa came to stand next to him. Without thinking, he reached out and slid an arm over her shoulders.

"It's all going to be alright. They'll be safe."

He knew better than to make such promises. Quickly, he said a silent prayer for their safety and asked for guidance to protect the woman at his side.

She might not have realized it yet, but by sending the baby and his family to Ohio, they'd just added fuel to the fire of the ringleader's anger and desperation.

And possibly his need to end Vanessa's life. Carter vowed to put himself between her and any danger. He'd gladly lose his life to save hers.

TEN

Carter hopped into the driver's seat and slammed his door.

"I grabbed a couple of water bottles from my trunk." He placed them in the cupholders. "They're not frozen, but very cold."

"I don't mind. Thanks." She opened hers and took a long swallow.

Carter started the engine and aimed the vehicle back to the main road. He had no destination in mind. He couldn't remember the last time he'd been this exhausted. At least he wouldn't be expected to go into the station for the next couple of days. However, he doubted he'd do much relaxing.

Not while Vanessa remained a name on someone's hit list.

They'd need to be proactive.

"We'll find a place for the night, get a hot meal. Then, I think we should begin making a list of women that might be targeted."

Vanessa opened her purse and pulled out a container of gum. She dumped a single cube into her palm. Scrunching her nose, she shook out another cube. "This has definitely been a double gum kind of day. Want some?"

He shook his head. "Nah. I can only chew gum until the flavor's gone. Then I'm looking for a way to get rid of it. Nothing is grosser than having wads of chewed gum in my truck."

Vanessa laughed.

He could listen to that sound every day. No, he wouldn't go there. Vanessa was part of a case, not his girlfriend.

His mind wandered over the events of the afternoon. The expression on her face after she'd delivered the baby flashed into his mind. He shouldn't ask. He knew it was asking for trouble. Curiosity proved too strong to resist.

"Vanessa?"

"Yes?" She popped the gum into her mouth and chewed, letting out a happy hum.

He smiled. She was so easily pleased sometimes, and others she was prickly. A woman like Vanessa Hall would keep a man on his toes, that's for sure.

He turned his gaze back to the road. "I wanted to ask you something, but I know it might cross the line into too personal. If it is, that's fine."

He hesitated, knowing that if he had to ask, it was probably not something he should ask.

"If it is, I won't answer."

Well, with that kind of answer, he decided to take a risk. "Okay. I noticed that when you handed the baby to Abigail, you had the strangest look on your face."

"Strange?" she asked quietly, her whole posture saying she was on high alert.

"Yeah. To me, it looked like you were both happy, and sad. I just wondered about it, but now that I'm asking, I think it's none of my business."

He retreated. Or tried to. Next to him, Vanessa stilled. Her throat worked. He became concerned.

"Look, I shouldn't have said—"

She placed a hand on his arm, halting his apology.

"I've never talked about it. Not to my parents. Not to my siblings. Not even to Darlene, my best friend."

His stomach knotted. He hadn't meant to tread into such private territory. "I didn't mean to hurt your feelings."

Why couldn't he keep his mouth closed?

"It's not that. I can't explain it, but I feel like I can tell you. Maybe because we have no history. You won't judge me. Or if you will, again, we don't have a relationship beyond this case."

That put him in his place. He wanted to protest, but what had she said that wasn't true? All he knew was she looked like she needed to tell someone. "If you want to tell me, I'm here. It won't go anywhere."

She sat for another full minute, thinking it through before she gave a single decisive nod. "I'll tell you, but please don't look at me."

The last four words sank to a throaty whisper. Carter kept his gaze on the road ahead.

"My family has always been a very devout one. I've always known what conduct was considered moral and what wasn't. I guess I started to rebel my senior year in high school. When I went away to college, my dream was to finish my bachelor-of-science degree in biology, then go on to veterinary medicine." She reached out and grabbed the water bottle. She twisted off the cap, then took another sip. "I met a guy there. Nolan. He was two years ahead of me. I knew immediately my parents wouldn't approve of him. He had 'bad boy' written all over him. And I fell head over heels, but didn't tell anyone in my family about him. He seemed so sweet, and I blamed my parents' restrictive beliefs for the fact that they wouldn't be able to see the sweetness in him."

His gut clenched tighter and tighter as she spoke. He already knew this story wouldn't have a happy ending. Suddenly, he recalled the tattoo he'd seen on her back and he wanted to tell her to stop.

Except she needed to tell this story. The bitter words that poured from her came from deep inside. She'd let them poison her heart long enough.

He cleared his throat. "Did they ever find out?"

"Oh, no. You see, even though I was rebellious enough to date him, I still knew certain behaviors were wrong. So I told Nolan my beliefs, and I thought he respected them."

A hollow laugh escaped, completely different from her previous laughter. This laugh cut and burned. "I was so naive. He had zero respect for me. We watched a movie at his house, and he drugged me. I was aware of what happened at some level, but when I woke up, I was too ashamed to do anything. When I found out I was pregnant, I actually told him. I don't know why. He didn't care. A month later, I miscarried."

Her voice caught. Carter couldn't stand it. He pulled the truck into a parking lot and stopped, keeping the engine running. He unbuckled and carefully gathered Vanessa into his arms. She didn't resist. He let her sob into his shoulder until her tears ran dry.

When she sat up, she wiped her face with her hands. "Sorry. I'm good now. You can drive."

He gave her a clean napkin. "Did you press charges?"

She blew her nose. "No. Who'd believe me? We were dating, and I'd willingly gone to his house."

"What he did was wrong."

"I know. It's taken a long time to learn to cope with it."

When he was sure she wouldn't start crying again, he buckled up and resumed driving. "It wasn't your fault. He was a snake. You were young. He's not worth any more of your time."

She gave a watery chuckle. "You're right there. I was so sunk in grief and shame, my grades tanked and I was this close to being put on probation." She held her thumb and index finger about a centimeter apart. "I'm sure my parents thought I was on drugs. There was no way I'd get into any vet program. I decided to go into the certified nurse midwife program. Partly because I wanted to help other women. But also because I felt so dirty. I couldn't trust my judgment in men, and frankly, I didn't see how I could trust one, so this was as close to motherhood as I would ever get."

Sadness welled up inside him. "Aww, Vanessa. You would make a great mother. Don't let him steal that from you."

She raised her head and those blue eyes pierced him. "That's not all he stole. I was so ashamed. So angry. I lost my faith."

Carter took his right hand off the wheel and reached over to squeeze her hand. "Vanessa, you haven't lost it. Maybe you were angry. Maybe you even ignored God for years. I remember you praying for Abigail on the way over. Your faith is still inside you. God is still there waiting for you, too."

Vanessa felt lighter than she had in years, regardless of the current circumstances. A killer was hunting her, and still a wild spark of joy ignited inside her.

She smothered it quickly, used to taking caution to the extreme. It had become a habit, but one that had spared her heartache.

And happiness.

She could live without romance. It wouldn't be fun, but it was possible. Living without God, though, she finally admitted to herself, had drained her.

"I've missed God in my life," she admitted, speaking out loud.

"That's no accident," Carter assured her. "God is calling you back to Him. No matter what we do, He'll never abandon us. The other side of that coin is that He won't force His love on us."

"So He'll accept me back, but it's up to me to make the first step."

"Well, isn't that fair? You were the one that left the relationship."

Relationship. That was the one thing. "I don't think I ever had a relationship with Him. We went to church. And I followed the rules."

"Did you ever take the time for private prayer?"

She frowned, then shook her head. "I always seemed too busy."

"Yeah. I get that. But imagine what kind of relationship you'd have with Darlene if you never talked with her."

She started to nod, then gasped, a new, horrifying thought occurring to her.

"What?"

"My family," she choked out. "I've been so ashamed, I didn't want them to find out. I've been pushing them away, too. What if I can't repair that damage?"

Carter had a poor relationship with his mom. But that was because of his mom's condition. He still strove to care for her and be there for her. Vanessa, though, had literally shoved away her family. Moving out of her parents' home, missing family gatherings, signing up to work on holidays even when she didn't have to.

"Hey. I'm sure that your family will welcome you back. I think you might have to tell them what happened to you, though."

She went cold. "I don't know if I can do that."

Carter's warm hand captured hers. "Vanessa, it wasn't your fault. What he did to you, it was date rape. And it's a crime."

"I know that! I also know I went out with exactly the type of boy my parents disapproved of."

Had she done it because she liked him, or because he was

what her parents had warned her against? She'd been so shallow, and so sure she knew better than them. After all, they were old-fashioned and uncool.

Only now, she saw that they had been wise and she'd fallen for a few pretty lines. Her vanity and pride truly had led to her own fall from grace.

Bright light flooded the truck cab. Vanessa raised an arm to cover her eyes, shrinking from the blinding beams.

Carter exclaimed and put the truck into Reverse. "I think he might be drunk. Hold on!"

The truck jolted backward. There was horrid screech when the rear bumper scraped along the guardrail. Carter didn't stop. He slid the vehicle into Drive, then pulled forward, spinning the wheel in an attempt to avoid the oncoming vehicle.

It was too late. The car T-boned the truck, striking it in the middle of the bed on the passenger side.

Two men jumped from the car. The moment she saw the gun in one of their grasps, Vanessa understood this wasn't a drunk driver. They were here for her.

She screamed at Carter. He leaped from his side, his Glock in his hand, and raced around the front of the truck. One of the men ran toward Vanessa. She slapped the door-lock mechanism, shaking when she heard it click.

Whoever had designed the vehicle to unlock when the driver's door opened, well, she was not a fan.

Carter shot the other attacker in his gun hand. The weapon flew from his grasp. Instead of giving up, the assailant flung himself on the lieutenant. Vanessa took her gaze from the second assailant to ensure Carter was fine.

The driver's-side window exploded. She whipped around. A bullet punched into her seat, inches from her head. The other attacker appeared at the driver's side. Reaching in through the shattered window, he unlocked the door. Then he was in the cabin, grabbing for her. His hands reminded her of claws. He attempted to drag her out of the cab. She resisted, bringing her feet up to kick out at him. One heel caught him in the jaw.

He flopped onto the road. Carter's opponent took one look at his felled partner and took off. He retrieved his weapon from the ground where Carter had kicked it and took aim. Carter ducked behind the door, still open from when the second assailant had tried to get to Vanessa.

Instead of shooting, the man took off toward his car and hopped in. The man Vanessa had knocked out jumped to his feet, whipping a knife from his pocket. He charged at Carter, screaming, the knife raised high.

Carter raised his gun and shot the man in the leg. Screaming, he flailed and fell to the ground. His howls changed into a low gurgle, then stopped.

His partner abandoned him and sped off in their car.

Carter approached the fallen man slowly. He gently rolled him onto his back.

He'd fallen on his own knife.

Vanessa saw his blank eyes a second before he dropped to the road and knew he was dead.

"We have to call this in." Carter picked up his phone and dialed. It only took a few words for her to realize he was talking directly with his chief.

Vanessa sat back in her seat, heart racing. Carter's voice soothed her.

"The coroner is on the way. So is backup. Should I have asked for a paramedic?" His brows furrowed as he glanced at her.

"No. I'm not hurt. Just a little freaked out."

Suddenly he chuckled. "The chief is also sending out a team to repair the window of my truck. So we won't have to freeze when we leave."

They sat in silence until the coroner arrived twenty minutes later. Backup arrived a few minutes later.

Vanessa waited in the other cruiser until the coroner left and the window repair team had completed the job. She glanced at the clock. They'd been sitting here for nearly two hours.

Finally, she and Carter were back on the road.

"Carter, he didn't try to kill me," Vanessa flipped her hair over one shoulder and braided it to give her hands something to do. "If they'd wanted me dead, why not just shoot both of us? Instead, the one who fell on his knife, he tried to drag me from the truck. Like he wanted to abduct me."

Carter shrugged. "I don't know. What changed? We need to find a safe place to hole up for the night and start working on that list."

"You're going to have a nice bruise." She gently touched the side of his jaw. Then she flushed and removed her hand.

"It's nothing serious. I don't know if you saw it, but one of them managed to get in a good jab before I stopped him."

"I hadn't noticed."

What worried her was the endless supply of people willing to commit crimes for money. When would she be safe?

Please, God, don't let him succeed. She thought of her family, and all the relationships she wanted another chance to reconcile.

And she thought of what Carter had said. Would she ever have the opportunity, or the bravery, to have another go at romance, and maybe have a child of her own one day?

The idea scared her. It also left her feeling sad. She didn't want to look too deeply into her emotions, but had a feeling that her confusion was rooted in the complex man seated so close to her.

ELEVEN

"How are you holding up?" Carter gave Vanessa a once-over. She looked tired, but he couldn't see additional physical injuries.

To his surprise, a laugh gurgled from her. Her blue eyes sparkled at him in the fading light. "That's getting to be your standard conversation starter. Asking me how I'm doing or if I'm hurt. It's not a good pattern."

He laughed, shaking his head. "I guess not, but you have to admit, we haven't had a good couple of days."

"True. You know, I'm rather proud of myself. I didn't know I could defend myself that well."

"Huh. You sound like that was a big accomplishment."

She tilted her head. "Wasn't it? They were both bigger than me. I honestly don't know how we've outsmarted them this many times."

"I think we've been very blessed."

Vanessa's smile wobbled than flipped into a puzzled frown. "I guess I've never considered my life in that light before."

She looked down at her clothes. "I don't want to complain, but do you think we could stop at a store? I need some things."

They stopped at a big-box store and stocked up on toiletries and some clothing items to get her through the next couple of days. She started to argue when he pulled out a credit card, until he glared her into silence.

"You are in the care of the SRPD," he murmured close to her ear. The light floral fragrance of her hair reminded him of spring. He liked it.

She shivered suddenly.

"Come on. You're cold. Let's get out of here." He headed to LaMar Pond. It was far enough away to give them some distance from Sterling Ridge, but still close enough to start their search in the morning. "We'll order a pizza or something equally healthy and get a working list. Then tomorrow, we can begin making the rounds to as many homes as we can."

"And I need to take my antibiotic while we eat."

"That too."

"Hopefully, the people around here will talk with us." She leaned against the back of the seat, rotating her head so she could still look at him while she talked. "At least you're not in your shiny police car. That wouldn't encourage friendliness."

Carter snorted. He couldn't help it. "I'm a very friendly guy. Why wouldn't anyone talk with me?"

They kept up the light banter all the way to the motel to cover up the fear flowing under the surface. Carter expected an attack to come out of nowhere at any moment. Only when they were in their rooms did he relax his vigilance, but only a little.

"This door," he said, switching it to the unlocked position, "connects our rooms. It will allow you to have your privacy, but if something happens, I'm going to be in the next room."

He placed the bag he kept packed and ready on the counter. In his line of work, he'd learned he needed to expect surprises and should be prepared to move out at any moment. That was also why he had an agreement with his mother's cousin that he could leave his mother with her at a moment's notice.

A knock on the door sent Vanessa scurrying to her room. Carter waited until the door between the two rooms had completely closed before he went to the door leading outside.

He paid for the pizza and tipped the delivery boy. He carried the box in one hand with a two-liter bottle of soda under his arm, then shut and locked the door. He frowned. Only one lock. He didn't like the wimpy security.

He'd sleep with his gun next to him tonight. If he managed to sleep at all. He'd probably sleep in his jeans and a T-shirt.

Carter flicked the curtain back. He scanned the parking lot. A beat-up little car with a pizza sign on the top departed from the lot. He dropped the curtain, then moseyed over to the connecting door and knocked.

"All clear, Vanessa. We have food."

"Coming." Vanessa undid the locks from her side and entered his room. She'd taken a minute to tie up her abundant hair in a high ponytail. The style suited her. It emphasized her high cheekbones and strong jawline.

Carter pivoted on his heel and set the pizza on the table. Glasses clinked near the sink. Soon, Vanessa sat down across from him and placed two glasses on the round table. She took her medication, then they dug into the pizza. It was hot and cheesy. The perfect meal for an exhausting day. For a few minutes they sat in silence as they ate.

When he'd finished, Carter threw away his paper plate and reached for a pen and a notebook he kept in his bag.

"Okay. I think we need to start with a list of families where the mother is due to have her baby within the next three months."

Vanessa wiped her mouth and took long swallow of the cold soda. "Why don't we start with those who will have their children the soonest, and work our way back from there?"

"We could, but it might be more efficient to list them geographically. That way we won't waste time backtracking all over northwestern Pennsylvania."

She tapped her bottom lip with her fork. He looked away, his face heating.

"We can do that, too. The list won't be that huge. Most Amish families in this area don't use medical centers unless there might be a complication."

By ten-fifteen, they had a list of ten women who were due anytime between the next week and mid-March.

They mapped out a route using the map feature on Carter's phone.

"I think we should visit Edna Lapp before—" Vanessa broke off and yawned widely. It was the fourth yawn in the past ten minutes.

"That's it." Carter capped his pen and closed the notebook. "You can barely keep your eyes open and I'm struggling not to slouch. Let's call it a night. We can head out tomorrow morning at eight, grab a bite on the way and reach the first house by eight thirty or eight forty-five. How does that strike you?"

Vanessa clapped her hands over her mouth to hide another yawn. "That's fine with me. I seriously need some sleep."

They both stood, nearly colliding. The air between them zinged with awareness. If he didn't distract himself, he'd end up doing something really stupid, like kissing her.

He shoved his fingers through his hair and moved to the connecting door.

When she walked through to her room, he suddenly realized she'd been out of it for hours. "Hold on. Let me check your room out."

"Oh, of course."

She waited while he made sure her space was secure. Before he left, he took the chair near her table and dragged it to the outer door and shoved the back of it under the doorknob.

"I really hope that's overkill." Her voice wasn't judgmental, merely matter of fact.

"Same. But I'd rather not take any chances. There's only one lock on the door here. If we haven't arrested this perp by tomorrow, we'll find a different location to stay for the night."

She frowned. "I hope this is all cleared up tomorrow. I only took off through then."

"I'm sorry. But I think saving your life needs to take precedence."

She gave in, thankfully.

He left her to go to his room and get some rest. Tomorrow would be a long day. Would they save a life?

Before he let sleep overtake him, he prayed the Lord would lead them to the next target so they could rob the adoption ring of another baby. He also prayed for the safety of Vanessa and himself.

Lastly, he pleaded with God. *Please, Lord, help me do my job without falling for this woman. She's exactly the kind of woman I'd dream of if I weren't so broken.*

But he was broken, and not a good match for such a strong and vibrant woman.

Vanessa stared at the connecting door for several minutes before she shook her head. This was ridiculous. Exhaustion blurred her mind. That was why she was acting this way. Vanessa never mooned over men. They didn't fit into her plan and that was it.

Resolutely, she spun away from the offending door and got ready for bed. She barely had enough energy to brush her teeth for a full two minutes, like she did every night. Still, nothing refreshed her the way clean teeth did.

When she finally crawled between the top sheet and the fitted one covering the full mattress, she expected to fall asleep very quickly. After all, she hadn't been this bone-tired in a long time.

She felt like she had experienced every emotion known to man in the last forty-eight hours. She craved the peace of oblivion to help her regain her perspective and clarity. And to strengthen her against temptation.

Had she really wanted Carter to kiss her a few minutes ago? That wasn't going to happen. Vanessa punched her pillow with gusto and rolled to her side. She pulled the covers up under her chin and snuggled into her pillow.

Unfortunately, sleep didn't come easily. Whether it was because her mind was racing too fast or because the bed was too soft, she didn't know. Maybe it was because of all the unsettling thoughts bubbling inside her brain, most of them centered on Carter. They were thoughts she had not let herself entertain in over seven years.

Then there were her feelings about what he'd said regarding her family. A new hope rose inside her, but it mingled with trepidation. She'd spent so long pushing away her parents, her brothers and her sister. How did she bridge that gap again? Honestly, she feared this time, they'd rebuff her.

Her family had never stopped loving her. She knew that. But they also had stopped pressing her. She hoped it was because they wanted to respect her and not because they decided it wasn't worth their time and energy.

Stop. She knew that wasn't true. Hadn't her mother sent her a card two weeks ago telling her she was praying for Vanessa and would be there if she ever wanted to chat?

And didn't Zach make a point of stopping by whenever he did a rotation that brought him in the area?

No, the family wasn't the issue. It was all her.

She also considered her new feelings about God. Briefly,

she tried to say a prayer, an honest prayer. It was hard after being silent for so long. She wasn't quite sure what to say.

God knew. She heard her dad's voice in her head.

Her father once told her the words you said when praying weren't important. God understood what was in your heart.

"God, I don't know how to build a relationship with You again. I'd like to try, though. Please help me."

Finally, she drifted off to sleep. The next morning came too soon. Christmas was officially seven days away. When Carter knocked on the door to wake her up, she bolted upright in the bed, her heart pounding. He called her name and she remembered where she was. Rubbing her eyes, she pushed back the covers and fumbled out of bed.

"I'm up," she called.

Vanessa stumbled into the shower and turned the water up as hot as it would go. Ten minutes later, she was dressed in casual, yet modest clothing. Knowing they were going to visit Amish homes today, she didn't bother with any of her makeup. She would have loved to have used a swipe of mascara or slicked on some of her trademark red lipstick. The bold color always bolstered her confidence. But today was not the day for boldness. She needed to go with simplicity. Therefore, she gathered her hair back and wound it up into a serviceable bun at the nape of her neck. When she peeked in the mirror at the final image, she laughed.

Some might not even recognize her as Vanessa Hall. She was fine with that. Today wasn't about her—it was about helping women, families and babies.

When Carter knocked on the door again, she was ready. She swung the door open and grinned when his eyes widened. Finally, he chuckled.

"You look good. You look like a woman ready to tackle the world."

She batted her eyelashes at him. "Thank you, sir. I am."

Within fifteen minutes, they'd checked out and were on their way. Carter had plugged the first address into the GPS system already.

"Tell me about this house."

She looked at the notes she had made the night before. "Virginia and Ben Hostetler. Virginia, or Ginny, is expecting her second child. Actually, she's expecting twins. That's why she came to the medical center. She was much sicker than she was with the previous baby. She was anemic. She's due in four weeks, but with twins, she'll deliver early. We'd talked about a caesarean section with the obstetrician on staff, but they were against it."

"Do you do them?"

She shook her head. "I'm not trained as a surgeon, but I can assist."

They pulled into the driveway of an immaculate farmhouse. It was white, as Amish houses in the area were. By the time they'd left the truck and had started toward the back door, where visitors entered, Ben Hostetler was already waiting, a small little boy standing next to him.

His closed expression warmed the moment he recognized Vanessa. "Vanessa! We weren't expecting you."

"Good morning, Ben." She smiled at the child. "Good morning, Ivan."

The youngster waved shyly then ducked behind his father.

"Mind if we come in for a minute? We have something to tell you and Ginny."

Ben welcomed them into his home. To her surprise, Ginny sat holding a newborn. Another woman rocked a second baby.

"Ginny! I didn't know you'd had your babies!"

The young woman grinned. "*Jah!* They surprised us and came early, two weeks ago."

She'd obviously had them at home.

"Has anyone been in to see them?" Her clinical eye swept over the sleeping children. They were tiny, as twins typically were, but otherwise seemed healthy.

"Our midwife has *cumme* several times to check on them. If you didn't know about them, why are you here?"

Vanessa introduced Carter and then let him explain their situation.

Ginny said something in Pennsylvania Dutch, the language the Amish used. It was a combination of English and German, and a sprinkling of words used only by the Amish.

Vanessa and Carter waited politely while they talked. Ginny finally turned to them.

"*Danke* for warning us. My *mamm* and sister are here to help me. We will move the babies so that an adult or two are always in the room with them."

"And you," Vanessa suggested softly. If the killer didn't know Ginny well, they might not realize that she had already had her baby. Her style of dress and apron disguised the fact that her babies had been born.

"*Jah*. I will always have someone with me. You will tell us when the danger is over, ain't so?"

The stern stare she fixed on them said she wasn't asking a question.

"We will," Carter assured the family.

The next house, they found no one home. Vanessa left a detailed message with the neighbor, who promised to speak with the family when they arrived home from visiting family in another district.

"Will they listen?" Carter asked.

Vanessa chewed on her bottom lip. "I really don't know. I wasn't the midwife who worked with Mary when she and her husband came into the clinic. She isn't due for another three months, though, so I suspect she probably won't be high on the kidnappers' list. We can circle back in a day or so, if he's still out there."

Her stomach churned. How long would this continue?

"Don't think about it." Carter's warm hand covered hers. Without thinking, she flipped up her palm up and threaded their fingers together. Then she blushed. When she tugged, he didn't immediately release her hand.

"I'm serious, Vanessa. We will do everything we can to protect these women and their babies. But we can't fix everything."

She stopped trying to rescue her hand. "How do you do it? How do you live with what you can't solve?"

He shrugged. "You don't have a choice. Not if you don't want to burn out. Or lose faith. Focus on the next task. In our case, focus on the next family."

They were able to visit five more families. One of them made plans to visit family, three of them promised to take precautions, but didn't outline what those were. They discovered the fifth family they visited had already had their baby, who'd been born prematurely with complications and was in the NICU for the foreseeable future.

"I'd say that was a good day's work," Carter announced when they got back into his truck. "I found a bed-and-breakfast about twenty miles from here. We'll go there for the night. I already booked two rooms."

She was too heartsick to argue. The kidnapper and Mandy's killer remained free. She was supposed to go into work in the morning but couldn't. Guilt attached her. She'd already taken off yesterday and today. But it couldn't be helped. When they stopped at the bed-and-breakfast, she used the phone at the front desk to call Shannon, the clinic's receptionist, and explain she'd still be out the next day.

"Oh? When do you think you'll be back?" her friend asked, avid curiosity in her voice.

"I'm going to say don't put me on the clock for the next week. After that, I'll let you know."

She'd miss four shifts.

"I wish you hadn't contacted them," Carter complained.

"I had to. I didn't want to get fired."

She could see he was tense about the call. But there was nothing to be done about it. The call had been made. It wasn't like she'd sent a text anyone could read.

And she trusted Shannon. But what if Shannon had a secret addiction she didn't know about?

Vanessa shoved away the fear. She'd known Shannon for years. She was quiet, conscientious and a devout Christian.

By the time she got into bed that night, she'd convinced herself that Carter had worried for no reason.

She closed her eyes and drifted off to sleep.

A noise woke her. The room was dark. She started to sit up. Someone moved.

A shriek built up in her throat. A strong hand covered her mouth, muffling her cry. "Don't do that. I won't hurt you. But you need to come with me quietly."

Cold sweat broke out on her brow.

She was being kidnapped.

Vanessa struggled in his grasp. For a moment, his arms loosened, and she thought she'd escape. A tiny prick in the fleshy part of her bicep made her gasp. She was being drugged!

She gave another feeble effort to tear away from him before she toppled over into blackness.

TWELVE

Something wasn't right.

Carter shoved his feet into his shoes and knocked on Vanessa's door. Outside, it was still dark. A glance at his watch told him it was just past four in the morning. She wouldn't be expecting him for another three and a half hours.

In his gut, he knew something awful had happened. He didn't know what woke him up, but he wasn't one to neglect his gut instincts.

Right now, they were screaming at him to check on Vanessa. When she didn't answer her door, a chill worked its way down his spine. He tried the door. It was locked. That didn't mean much. These doors locked the moment you shut them. He'd found that out the night before when she'd locked herself out and he'd laughingly gone and gotten the spare key. He'd obtained two keys for both of their rooms, so they could enter either room in an emergency.

He ran back to his room, snarling under his breath at the waste of precious seconds, and snagged the extra keys from the nightstand beside his bed. Why hadn't he grabbed them when he first went to check on her?

Because the fog hadn't lifted from his brain yet. He knew it, but still, he castigated himself for not thinking clearly.

At her door, he fitted the lock into the keyhole and turned

the knob. The room was empty. He knew it even before he hit the light switch on the wall.

Every instinct urged him to rush out to his truck and chase her down. Find her.

Fortunately, his training kicked in. He scanned the room for any dangers. Once he saw the room was clear, he focused on figuring out what had happened. It didn't take long. Her bed had been slept in. The state of the sheets suggested a struggle.

On the floor next to the bed, he found a discarded syringe. She'd been drugged.

No wonder he didn't hear her struggle or call. Vanessa wouldn't hesitate to scream if she could. No, they'd tranquilized her.

He recalled their conversation about the motives changing. The abduction ring seemed to want her alive. They hadn't tried to kill her when they'd rammed into his truck. That certainty settled into his soul and helped calm the rage burning in his blood.

"I need to be smart. Vanessa is alive. I will find her."

How? He needed help. He still believed someone at the force might have been feeding the killer information.

Brett. He could trust Brett.

Without another thought, he dialed his best friend, uncaring that he'd be waking him from sleep in the middle of the night. He and Brett had always come to each other's aid, no matter time or weather.

Brett answered on the third ring. "Yeah? What do you need? Is it your mom?"

For a second, Carter couldn't speak around the emotion tightening his throat. He cleared it twice. "No. My mom's fine. But, Brett, I need your help."

He thought about telling Brett to keep it quiet. But if they already had Vanessa, saving her life took priority. Which meant he needed to use what resources were available.

"Let me explain what's been happening." He took Brett through the past few days succinctly, trying, and almost succeeding, to keep to the facts without letting any of the emotions roiling inside him to escape.

"You think Shannon, the receptionist, might have been helping the kidnapper?"

"It's a possibility we can't ignore. I'm also curious how he got into Vanessa's room. How did he know which was hers?"

"This is what we're going to do," Brett decided. "You work on that end, see if you can find where Vanessa is or how she was taken. I'm going to head that way and meet up with you."

"That works."

"I'm also going to rope in another cop. Who do you think? Someone to check out the clinic receptionist?"

Carter allowed himself a few seconds to sift through the other cops at the department. "Let's call in Ryan."

"Yeah. That's who I'd go with, as well."

"I'm also going to call the chief on her personal line. I don't know who the leak at the police station is—"

"Wait, what?" Brett exclaimed. "I knew something shady was going down when you used our code, but, dude, we have a leak?"

"Sorry. I meant to update you on that, too. Yes. I'll tell you when you arrive."

They hung up and Carter focused on the tasks he'd taken on. He went down to the front desk. No one was behind it. That was odd. He leaned forward. A shoe stuck out.

Going around the desk, he found the desk clerk out cold. A syringe like the one he'd seen in Vanessa's room was lying on the rug near the man. So the kidnapper had drugged the clerk.

Carter contacted 911 and requested an ambulance. By the

time the paramedics arrived, he'd figured out how the kidnapper had found Vanessa.

He let them take charge of the unconscious clerk and stepped out into the night air. Then he called Chief Kaiser. Brett walked up as they were talking. He put the chief on speaker.

"Brett's here, too, Chief." He nodded at his friend, smiling his gratitude. "I have you on speaker."

"Great. So the kidnapper drugged the night clerk. How did he get the guest room list?"

"I'm speculating that he had him bring up the list, either by threatening him or by tricking him, I don't know which. And when he had what he needed, he either picked the lock or there was another key available. I found another syringe in the room, so Vanessa is probably in the same condition as the clerk."

Here, he had to pause. She'd been drugged before, made vulnerable in the most horrific way. Would this traumatize her beyond her ability to cope? No. He couldn't go there.

"Chief, this is Talbot," Brett said, entering the conversation. "I got off the phone with Lieutenant Douglass just before I arrived. We'd wondered if the medical clinic's receptionist had been responsible for leaking Vanessa's location. I think she's been cleared. It seems she posted Vanessa's absences, then clocked out for the night. She left the clinic. Someone went in after hours and checked the number last called."

"Is that who kidnapped her?"

"We don't know, ma'am. It was either the kidnapper or the person who hired him. But I'm pretty sure after tonight that whoever is behind this works at the clinic."

"I'm on it. I need to get a warrant for a list of employees. I'll present it to the judge first thing this morning."

"Any news on finding the leak?" Carter rubbed at the ache forming in the back of his neck.

"About that. I found that one of our interns is dating one of the paramedics. Apparently, they were chatting on the radio, on a public channel, about things they shouldn't have been. Vanessa's car was mentioned, because it had been a rather exciting event, and the intern mentioned you'd be over to reclaim it with her. They're both relieved of duty until we decide what to do with them. At the very least, there will be a formal reprimand in their files."

They'd broken confidentiality and put his and Vanessa's lives on the line. Carter ground his teeth, holding in the acidic comments he wanted to say. He needed to keep his attention on the goal.

"We need to circulate a picture of Vanessa and begin to search." Carter tightened his fingers around his phone.

"I'm calling in all available officers. With her red hair, she'll stand out."

He hoped so.

Every minute they stood around talking she got farther away from him. He ended the call and pocketed his phone, nodding once to Brett.

"Let's move." His heart pounded in his chest so hard, it ached. He couldn't do anything about that. All he could do was pray that God would grace them with the skills to find Vanessa and bring her safely home.

No other option was acceptable.

Vanessa stirred, her muscles heavy, like they were weighted down. Even her eyelids didn't want to cooperate.

The surface under her cheek was hard and cold. It shook, jostling her tired body. The movement made her nauseous. Was she on a train? In a car?

Her body wanted to return to sleep. She couldn't allow that to happen. She forced herself to think. What had happened?

Gradually, the memories stirred. Someone had been in her room. She'd been given a shot that had knocked her out. She gagged and tasted bile. Someone had used a drug on her. Again. Fury and despair warred in her heart. She had told herself never again but hadn't been able to stop it.

Be not afraid. The words formed in her mind. It was a bible verse. Which one, she didn't know, but it didn't matter. She clung to the verse with all her heart. *Lord, I will trust You. I will try not to fear. Help me.*

She swallowed down her panic and took in a deep breath. She needed to see who had taken her. Once she had more information, she'd be better able to fight back and defend herself.

She forced her rebellious eyelids to crack open.

Daylight streamed down on her, through a small window. Her mind sharpened. The cut-out square window was centered near the top of a black metal box. As carefully as she could, she lifted her head and glanced around.

Vanessa blinked. Was she dreaming? She pinched herself. She was awake and riding in the back of an Amish buggy. A thick blanket covered her from her neck all the way down to her toes. She checked herself out for any injuries and was shocked to find that she wasn't bound in any way. Nor had she been harmed. She remained dressed in the same T-shirt, flannel shirt and sweatpants she'd worn to bed the night before. Even her thick woolen socks remained on her feet.

She'd have to acquire footwear if she meant to make a run for it. And she definitely planned on escaping.

She sighed, then pressed her fist against her mouth. She didn't want to alert the buggy driver that she was no longer unconscious. If he knew, that would blow any chance she'd have to get out of this situation.

Easing up on her elbow, she peered to the front of the buggy. And got another shock.

Her abductor was young and unfamiliar. That wasn't what surprised her. No, her astonishment was because the driver of the buggy was a young Amish man. One who, if she wasn't mistaken, was shaking more than the vehicle he was driving.

She heard a strange keening sound emerge from him. For a moment, she was stumped. Then, understanding struck. This young man who had drugged her and carried her out to his buggy in the middle of the night was weeping.

Vanessa knew regret when she saw it.

What did the kidnappers have on him to convince him to do this horrible deed? Because unless she missed her guess, he hadn't done it willingly.

"*Gott* forgive me," he moaned.

Forgive him for what? She waited to see if he'd confess anything more. He didn't say another word, though.

She settled back and waited. There was no back door on the buggy. Her only option would be to go out the door near the front, right behind the bench. That wasn't going to happen while the buggy was moving. Or while he sat there.

Which meant she needed to wait until the buggy stopped and he got down. Sweat beaded on her brow. How likely was it that he'd stop before reaching the final destination, whatever that was? Would he deliver her directly to the villain responsible for all the death and horror?

Her other concern was how far would they drive? She had no idea where they were, or how far they'd traveled. It was the middle of the night when they left. Judging by the light, it was between six thirty and seven in the morning now. She could tell that the sun hadn't completely breached the horizon. Had they traveled by buggy all that time?

Buggies sometimes traveled at night, but many drivers

chose not to because they didn't want to put the necessary lights on the vehicles. All these factors were making her head ache.

They bounced along for a stretch of time. She wasn't sure if it was ten minutes or an hour. The entire right side of her body felt like one large bruise due to the rough ride. Tears dripped out of the corners of her eyes.

The driver clucked. The buggy slowed and came to a stop, swaying slightly. Booted footsteps jumped from the bench and trod along the ground.

Away from the buggy.

Vanessa's heart leaped into her throat. He was leaving her alone. She sat up and glanced around. He walked into a barn.

No one else stood nearby. This was her only chance.

Vanessa threw off the blanket, clumsily tripping on the material in her haste. She crawled to the front of the buggy and dropped to the ground, hunching low, trying to keep out of sight.

Anyone coming along would see her hair. She grabbed the blanket and whirled it around her. She'd use it until she could find another way. She ran away from the barn that her reluctant abductor had disappeared into. Her stockinged feet grew sodden and cold as the snow melted.

She kept moving.

Using the blanket made traveling difficult. It dragged the ground, collecting snow and snagging on branches and rocks. She stumbled several times, falling to her knees. Soon, she trembled with cold. Her breath puffed in front of her face. She wasn't used to running.

Within minutes, a cramp worked its way into her side. She pressed one hand into it, trying to control the spasms, but kept running.

She raced across a road, startling a young Amish woman.

"Oh! Are you hurt?"

Vanessa had decided to run past the woman, but at her kind question, the sobs she didn't know she'd been holding in exploded from her. "Please. I've been kidnapped. I need to go home, but he'll find me. My hair..."

She couldn't say any more.

"Cumme."

The woman took her cold hand and pulled her into the barn. "Wait here." She sprinted out of the barn.

Vanessa hesitated. Wait, or leave?

A few minutes later, the woman returned. She had a pair of sturdy boots, socks, a long black cloak and—best of all—a stiff black bonnet. "Put these on. Your feet will be warm, and the man chasing you will not recognize the blanket or see your hair. He'll think you are Plain."

Vanessa tossed aside the soaked socks and blanket and dressed. The woman helped her pin her hair up then shoved the bonnet into place. Vanessa had never realized that the bonnets were so inflexible, like cardboard. The cloak went around her shoulders.

She wasn't completely warm, but she could run like this. "Thank you!"

"Go! I will pray for you!" the woman said. "Keep going east. You'll head toward the main part of town."

Vanessa would remember her kindness forever. She ran, trying to figure out where she was. Using the sun for a reference, she headed in the direction she thought was east. If she went far enough, she was bound to run into a business and could call Carter or the police.

It was her only hope.

Her legs trembled as she continued to walk. She forced herself to keep going. Every time she heard horse hooves clopping along the road, she left the main road and tried to hide until the buggy had gone past. Maybe it was overkill, but how many Amish women wore sweatpants?

She supposed she could be mistaken for a teenager, but she'd rather be ultracareful.

Sweat trickled down her back. Her stomach growled. She was so thirsty, she could barely swallow. If someone ordered her to spit, she might not be able to gather enough saliva to comply.

Up ahead, she saw a police cruiser brake at a stop sign. When she saw the words Sterling Ridge Police Department on the side of the vehicle, she stumbled to a halt, barely able to process that she had seen it. She watched the cruiser turn on the road and parallel-park beside a parking meter. The doors opened.

Her breath caught when Lieutenant Brett Talbot emerged from the driver's side and headed into the café he'd parked in front of.

Then she gasped. Carter stepped from the passenger side. He glanced both ways and then crossed the road.

"Carter," she whispered. Then she yelled, "Carter!"

He whipped around, his gaze scanning the street. "Vanessa?"

He didn't recognize her. Laughing, she tore the black bonnet off and ran toward him. She was ten feet from him when he swung toward her.

A grin split his face in two. "Vanessa!"

She slammed to stop inches from him, putting her hands on his arms to steady herself so she wouldn't fall over.

He didn't seem to mind.

Joy blazed in his eyes a second before he tipped up her chin, bent down and kissed her.

Vanessa's brain froze. She forgot why she shouldn't kiss him and returned the kiss, never wanting to stop.

THIRTEEN

She had never experienced a kiss that filled her with such joy. Vanessa lost herself in the moment. In fact, she forgot that they were standing in the middle of a public street, where anyone could see them.

Until a discreet throat-clearing reminded her that they weren't alone.

She and Carter broke apart. She cast a quick glance at him. His face and ears were red, too. He ducked his chin and rubbed his mouth.

She couldn't meet his gaze.

Glancing around to see who had cleared their throat, she was mortified to find Lieutenant Talbot standing two feet away, an amused smirk twisting his mouth.

"Oops." Carter backed away from her. He dropped his gaze, shoving a hand through his hair. "Sorry. I don't know what I was thinking."

The apology drained the rest of the euphoria from their shared embrace. Her guard went up again instinctively.

She forced a chuckle. "Um, you were probably thinking 'yay, she's not dead!'"

He cracked a smile, still looking embarrassed. "There is that. It really scared me, how easily you were taken."

He scanned her again. It was an assessing look. He was

worried that the event had set her back, she realized. But he wouldn't ask her in front of Brett. Some of her irritation faded at the obvious care and respect.

Then his gaze zeroed in on the bonnet still in her grasp. "I didn't recognize you at first."

She opened her mouth to explain, but her stomach took that minute to growl like a bear coming out of hibernation. Could this morning get any more embarrassing? However, she was alive, she'd found Carter and, for the moment, she was safe. That was worth a little embarrassment.

That kiss, too, had been worth a little mortification. It could never happen again. If his expression said anything, it told her that he regretted his impulsive reaction. But she would savor it, even if it was a once-in-a-lifetime experience. She would never forget it. Her lips continued to tingle from the touch of his.

"You need to eat," Carter proclaimed, seeming relieved to have something to do.

Her stomach growled a second time in agreement.

"We also need to know what happened," Brett added. The amusement had fled, replaced by a no-nonsense expression. He was back in police mode.

She nodded. Then frowned, cutting her gaze to Carter. "I thought you were going rogue for a few days. Apparently, that's changed."

He placed a hand on the small of her back and urged her toward the café that Brett had recently vacated. "Yeah. Brett and I are working together. The chief tells me she found the leak. While information had been shared that should not have been, it wasn't a malicious deed. But I'll explain it after we are sitting somewhere and you've ordered breakfast."

She knew that tone. Carter was in full protective mode. She gave in gratefully. Carter asked for a table in the back of the café. No other customers sat there. They would have privacy to discuss the events and to plan their next step. They kept the conversation general until she had a plate of pancakes smothered in syrup and a steaming mug of coffee with French vanilla creamer and a packet of sweetener.

She took an appreciative sip of the coffee and sighed.

Carter made a disgusted face, his own boring black coffee cradled in his palms. Brett noisily slurped Pepsi through a straw. The waitress brought him a refill with a flirtatious smile. He didn't seem to notice as he thanked her and accepted the icy drink. This one, he sipped at a slower pace.

Vanessa was ravenous. For a few minutes, the two officers allowed her to eat in silence. When her stomach felt pleasantly full, she took a last bite of one fluffy pancake, humming happily as the syrupy goodness hit her taste buds. She washed it down with sip of coffee, then pushed aside her plate aside.

"Are you done?" Carter looked at the remaining pancake with concern.

"I'm full. Honest." She placed a hand over her belly, feeling content. "I can never eat more than two and these were huge."

He nodded. "Good. Can you tell us what happened?"

She took another sip of coffee to fortify herself. "I don't know how he got into my room. I woke up because I heard something. A man was in my room. He drugged me." She couldn't stop the shudder that racked her body at the memory of the needle piercing her arm.

Carter's hand caught hers. "Take your time. We're here. You're safe."

She squeezed her eyes closed for a moment, then relaxed. "I'm fine. He didn't hurt me."

That reminder soothed away her fear.

He removed his hand. She missed it but forced herself to

continue. "When I woke up, I was confused at first. Then I realized I was in a buggy."

"What?" Brett blurted, setting his glass on the table with a loud clunk. Pepsi sloshed over the edge and splashed on the table.

"My kidnapper was a young Amish man. Probably early twenties." She told them everything she remembered about him and her escape. When she got to the part about being cold and wet, Carter broke in. "I have your stuff in the cruiser. You'll want to change into dry things."

She nodded. Getting into her own clothes would be a relief. Plus, the bottoms of her sweatpants were still damp from tromping around the countryside in the snow. "That's about it. I ran until I saw you."

The memory of his greeting surged to the front of her brain.

They both flushed and looked down.

Carter cleared his throat.

"I don't know why I woke up, but I knew something was wrong." Carter told her about finding the syringes and desk clerk. When he'd brought her up-to-date on everything that happened on his end, the trio sat in silence for a moment.

"You know, being in a buggy, you probably weren't taken as far as if your kidnapper had hired someone with a car." Brett wiped up the soda he'd spilled with a napkin.

"I thought of that," she murmured. "I wonder what the person behind all this used to force the young Amish man's compliance. It was clear to me he regretted his part."

"I want to know where he stopped." Carter added more coffee to his mug from the carafe the waitress had left them. "Was it his home? Had he made plans to meet someone there?"

By *someone*, she knew he meant the person who hired him. She still couldn't figure out why he needed her. Not that she wasn't glad that he seemed intent on abduction rather than murder, at least for now, but her stomach knotted regardless. The pancakes now felt like a solid lump inside her stomach.

"What now?" she finally asked, needing to move the conversation along to get her mind of her personal stalker.

"We're waiting for the chief to call," Brett informed her. "She is trying to find out more on how your kidnapper knew where you'd be."

She looked at Carter. "Did my call to Shannon do it?"

If Shannon was in on it, she'd lose all faith in her ability to judge people.

He nodded. "Afraid so. But I don't think Shannon is connected to it."

That was a relief. She really liked Shannon. If Shannon was innocent of any attempt to harm her, once this was in the past, she'd make time to get to know her more. Maybe it was time to expand her friend circle.

Beyond Darlene, that is.

Carter continued speaking. "We will have more information once the chief calls. In the meantime, I think we should continue our search. But we need to keep an eye open for the young man who kidnapped you. He needs to be questioned."

"I don't think he acted willingly," she reminded them.

"I understand that, but he did kidnap you. He had to have a reason." Carter held her gaze until she nodded. Brett took the bill and went up to pay.

"We'll meet you in the cruiser," Carter told him.

She saw the glance they exchanged. That was obviously bro code for Carter wanted a moment to talk with her alone. She sighed, already knowing that they were going to discuss the kiss.

She followed him out to the cruiser. When he opened the

back door, she scrunched up her face. "So I get to ride in the back like a criminal."

"Sorry. There's not room up front for all three of us." He pointed to the console area, which was full of gadgets.

"Excuses, excuses."

He hesitated, clearly trying to think of the right words.

"If you apologize for kissing me again, I'm going to scream."

He blinked at her, his mouth falling open. He closed it with a click. "I was going to. It wasn't appropriate."

"No, it wasn't. It was, however, a genuine reaction for two people who have been under a lot of stress and had honest reasons to doubt that I'd find you again. I thought I was going to die. I was so relieved to see you and realize I was safe again."

"It can't happen again."

She rolled her eyes. "Duh. I know that. Can we move on?"

It was hard to act nonchalant when a part of her heart was breaking. That kiss hadn't been merely relief for her. She wouldn't have kissed anyone but Carter that way. But she wouldn't tell him that. That would only lead to more disappointment.

He should be glad she was willing to forget and move on.

Carter found, however, that her casual attitude irritated him. That embrace had meant something, even though he knew it had been wrong. He'd never in all his adult life wanted to kiss a woman the way he'd kissed her. Her presence was a constant distraction. Her safety consumed his thoughts.

He'd done what he'd always said he wouldn't and fallen for her. That kiss had come from the depth of his feelings for her, and only her.

The fact that it didn't seem to mean as much to her burned.

Wasn't this what he wanted? He knew he was in no position for romance. Not with his duty to his mother. He certainly couldn't afford to become distracted now, not when her very life depended on his thinking clearly.

Holding in his annoyance, he moved to the back of the cruiser and lifted the hatchback door. "I have your stuff. You'll want to get into dry clothes."

She held out her hands. "Gimme."

He couldn't stop the smile that spread over his lips. She might have broken his heart a little, but she was so vibrant and sassy. He'd been so concerned that last night's abduction would damage her. But she seemed to have bounced back.

"Okay." He tossed the bag to her and watched her stride back into the café without a backward glance. *Lord, I can deal with a broken heart as long as she survives and I know she's in the world, healthy and whole.*

He closed the trunk and followed her inside. He was going to be extra careful from now on. Carter waited outside the bathroom while she changed, ignoring Brett's curious gaze.

Vanessa exited and grinned at him. "It feels so good to be out of my pajamas and into jeans again. I feel almost human."

"Awesome. Let's motor." He led the way back to the cruiser.

Brett sauntered out of the café. He met Carter's gaze. Carter dipped his chin. Yes, the necessary conversation had happened, although he was far from satisfied with the results. He closed the back door then ducked into the front passenger seat.

"Where to?" Brett asked, starting the engine.

Carter pulled out the list he'd made with Vanessa. It seemed like a lifetime ago that they'd sat in a hotel room discussing possible targets. "I think we need to adjust our plans."

"What do you mean?" she asked from the back seat.

He half turned in his seat so he could see Vanessa. "I suggest we search the homes close to where you escaped. That makes more sense, don't you agree? I'm hoping you'll see the man who kidnapped you. He might tell us who hired him."

She bit her thumb fingernail while she thought. "I know what you're saying, but I doubt he'll be able to tell us much. That seems to be the way this killer works."

"True. However, if we find out what the killer held over him to force his compliance, we might learn something new that will help us solve this case."

Vanessa shrugged. "You're the investigator. I'm game with whatever. I should warn you, though, I have no idea how far I ran. For a large part of it, I was so panicky, I don't know that I'll recognize the landscape. I did travel pretty much straight east."

"Then we'll go west." Brett flicked on his turn signal and pulled the cruiser onto the road.

Carter hated to think of what Vanessa had gone through. He forced himself to remain vigilant and not dwell on her abduction. It served no purpose. She was safe and well.

Every once in a while, Vanessa would point out something she remembered. Carter and Brett followed each comment with questions to target which direction she was facing, or where she'd come from when she saw the landmark.

Brett purposely drove under the speed limit, giving her more time to process what she saw. Several cars passed them when they were in a passing zone. It nearly made him smile. It wasn't often you saw people brave enough to pass a police cruiser on a two-lane road.

"Wait!" Vanessa shouted, surging forward in her seat to sit near the edge.

Carter jumped at the sudden yell.

Brett put his blinker on and pulled over. He punched the button to activate the hazard lights.

"What do you see?" Carter asked, keeping his tone soothing.

"That house." She pointed at a white house on the left side of the road. "That's the house where I stopped at. The one where the girl gave me the bonnet and the cloak."

She took a deep breath. Her finger trembled as she pointed toward the barn. "I left the blanket I'd taken from the buggy in there."

"Wait here."

Carter left her and Brett in the running vehicle. He picked up the clothes and the blanket that the Amish woman gave her. Then he grabbed an empty bag from the trunk and then jogged across the road. He shifted the items so it was all in his left hand. When he knocked on the door, a young woman answered.

"*Jah?* Can I help you?" Her voice, while respectful, was cautious.

"Yes. Ma'am, earlier today you helped a woman who'd been kidnapped."

Her gaze flared wide open. "Is she safe?"

"Yes. But we need to find out who attacked her. And I need the things she arrived in." He held out the blanket and clothes. "Also, I want to return these to you. You saved her life. Thank you."

"*Gut.* I'm glad." She took the items from him and set them on a table inside the door. "I left her things in the barn. I wasn't sure what to do with them. Let me get my boots on and I will show you."

She was as good as her word. Within five minutes, she'd led him to the place where Vanessa had dropped her socks and the blanket. He wrapped both in the garbage bag he'd taken from the car. He doubted any useful evidence could be gathered from the blanket, but he would follow procedure and turn it in. He'd do everything possible to ensure this perp was caught and buried in a jail cell for the rest of his natural life. Only then could he feel sure that when he walked out of Vanessa's life, she'd be able to be safe and flourish.

He couldn't think about what his life would look like without her in it. That wasn't the important issue right now.

After thanking the young woman, he strode to the cruiser and dumped the bag filled with the wet blanket into the back, making sure it was completely sealed.

Then he ambled around and climbed into the shotgun seat. "I have the blanket. And your socks. I talked with her a little bit. She didn't recognize the blanket. And you apparently hadn't told her about who took you."

Vanessa screwed up her mouth in distaste. "It felt awkward. I'm not used to sharing personal information. And I didn't want to tell her that the man was Amish. Call me strange."

"Nope. Not going to do that." Carter glanced down at the list in his hand. "She wasn't sure which direction you came from. However—"

He broke off when the young woman raced across the road to the cruiser.

Brett rolled down the window.

"Please," she gasped, holding her arm across her stomach. "I told *Mamm* about what happened. You told me some Amish women and babies were being kidnapped, ain't so?"

"Yes." Carter sat forward, sensing a break in the case.

"*Mamm* said that one of the local girls went missing two days ago. Maybe you should go see her family."

FOURTEEN

Vanessa's heart threatened to pound its way out of her chest. Another missing woman couldn't be a coincidence.

Brett and Carter both seemed to agree.

"Barbara Miller. She's not on our list." Carter frowned. His gaze met hers. She saw the question in them.

"That doesn't mean anything. Remember, not all Amish women use the clinic or go to see a doctor."

"Let's not get our hopes up." Brett maneuvered the cruiser into a driveway. "This might be a wild-goose chase. She might have run away or there might be a hundred other reasons why she's gone missing. This world can be an ugly place."

Vanessa winced at the cynicism running through his words. Brett had obviously seen his share of evil. Her gut told her this missing woman held an important key.

However, she wasn't in law enforcement, even if she did have a brother with the FBI. But Tanner would tell her that just because she didn't see a connection not to ignore that there might be a hidden one.

"We will never know until we talk with the family."

The three of them left the cruiser. Carter's arm brushed hers. It was amazing how much that simple touch comforted her. Hyperaware of his presence at her side, she moved toward the steps on the side of the house.

"Vanessa, why don't you begin the conversation?" he whispered. "I think they'll trust you more."

She nodded. She'd thought the same thing.

After wiping her damp hands on her jeans, she raised one and rapped her knuckles on the door. Then she took a deep breath. She should pray. It still felt awkward, but she quickly sent a silent prayer for help in finding the right words.

A young boy, maybe around fifteen, opened the wooden door and stared at her through the screen door. He didn't say anything, just waited for her to state her purpose. Carter stopped directly behind her. The boy's gaze widened.

"Hello. My name is Vanessa." He didn't nod or acknowledge her greeting in any way. She changed tactics. "Are your parents home?"

He shut the door in her face. She blinked. That had never happened before. She heard voices inside the house. A minute later, the door opened again. She found herself facing a much older version of the boy, his dark beard lightly sprinkled with gray.

"Jah?"

She needed to take care with her words. "Sir, I understand you have a daughter missing."

His face lost all expression. His eyes, though, were grief-stricken. She had to talk fast before the door slammed on her again for good.

She held up her hands in a placating motion. "There have been several kidnappings among the Amish communities lately. Please. We think your daughter might be the victim of the man we're searching for."

Hope and fear fought for dominance in his face. Finally, he nodded. "*Cumme.* My wife is in the kitchen."

The kitchen was bright and airy. Sunlight streamed in through windows on two walls, unhindered by curtains or blinds. Its happy appearance was contradicted in the moods of the people who joined them around the table.

Mrs. Miller looked as if she'd cried for days. Her hands twisted her apron in her lap while she listened to her husband.

"Our oldest daughter, Barbara. She vanished without warning two mornings ago. She went out to do her chores. We found the milking pail tipped over. And we found one of her boots. Nothing more."

Here was the delicate part. How to ask people whose culture didn't openly discuss pregnancy if their unmarried daughter could be expecting?

Mrs. Miller spoke up. "Her boyfriend has been distraught."

"Has he?" Carter murmured. "Have you seen him lately?"

Both parents froze at his tone.

Mr. Miller shook his head in denial. "Martin is a *gut* man. He wouldn't have hurt my Barbara."

"We weren't suggesting he would," Vanessa assured them. "But he might have heard Barbara talk about someone who had bothered her, or something she'd seen that might help us."

They relaxed, their hackles smoothed.

"He might have. Barbara told him everything. They have been walking out for nearly a year. I expect they will marry next fall."

If they find her alive. The thought hovered in the air, but no one wanted to say it. Tension was thick.

"Now that I think," Mr. Miller said, his voice trembling, "Martin was here yesterday morning. He promised he'd find her. Said something about sacrificing anything for her. Maybe he had a plan?"

His voice broke. He turned his face away, swallowing.

Invisible fingers squeezed Vanessa's heart. The poor man was close to collapse.

"Can you give us his address? Maybe we could talk with him. It might help us locate Barbara." Brett hadn't entered the conversation until now.

New hope dawned on their faces. "*Jah!* Of course."

Mrs. Miller rattled off the address. She then gave precise directions to Martin's home. "He lives alone. His family is not from this district. He'd just moved into the *haus* two years ago."

Brett and Carter stood. Vanessa thanked the Millers before rising to join them.

They didn't speak until they were safely in the cruiser again.

"What do you think?" Carter drummed his fingers on the window.

Brett shrugged. "I don't know. We should definitely go talk with this young man. He may or may not be the one who tried to take Vanessa."

"I, for one, have no doubt," Vanessa informed them. "But I am confused."

"About what?" Carter shifted to look at her.

For a brief moment, she lost track of her thoughts. Then she broke the link between them.

"First, Mandy's killer kidnaps babies. Until recently, he stuck to taking newborns. Both of the women he tried to abduct, Opal at the clinic and Abigail, the woman who got away from him at the market, were both very close to delivery."

"I'm with you. Go on."

She tugged on a red curl that had come loose from her bun. "I'm not sure what I'm getting at. It just seems something has changed. Not that I am complaining, but why take me when before he wanted me dead? And if it's the same person responsible for Barbara's disappearance, what's the motive? Unless she's expecting and her parents don't know it."

Such situations have happened before, but they were very rare.

Brett tapped his knuckle on the steering wheel. "None of this makes any sense."

It didn't take long to travel from the Miller house to Martin's home. Vanessa looked at the home and sucked in a breath. She wrapped her arms around her waist and held on tight as if she could keep the shudders wracking her body in.

"Vanessa?"

Carter's voice seemed far away.

"This is it. This is the place I escaped from this morning."

The man who had kidnapped her was so close. Soon, they may have all the answers. She knew it, but at the same time, she fought the desire to run and never come back.

Carter opened her door. Vanessa emerged from the vehicle with care, almost like she feared she'd break if she moved too fast. He watched her struggle to maintain her composure. Distress flickered on and off like the lights he strung on the Christmas tree in his living room.

He needed to maintain his professionalism. After all, even if he was off duty and dressed in blue jeans, he was still a cop. And they weren't alone. Brett was with him, and somewhere on the premises, they hoped to find Martin, the young man who had, either willingly or under duress, kidnapped her from her room in the wee hours of the morning, subjecting her to more trauma. Not just mentally, either. She hadn't said anything about physical suffering, but Carter was paid to be observant. He'd seen her rub at her side and grimace several times. She'd been trapped on the floor of a buggy with nothing to cushion her from the bumps.

"Are you ready?" he whispered. "Can you come with us? Or should we wait here and let Brett start searching?"

He knew Brett heard his question. When he glanced at his partner, he saw his concern mirrored on his friend's face.

Vanessa didn't like to display vulnerability. By the time he looked her way again, the distress he'd seen had been replaced with determination.

"I can do this." She straightened her spine. Her jaw tightened. If he listened closely, he imagined he'd be able to hear her teeth grinding. As a group, the three began walking toward the house. Carter had the absurd desire to place an arm around her. For what? She was fine, walking between two police lieutenants who both had loaded Glocks in their weapon holsters.

Ignoring the impulse, he used his radio to call into the station, letting the chief know they'd arrived at the suspect's house and were approaching.

"Take no risks. Keep me informed. Backup is ready at your request."

Carter agreed. Then he silently motioned to Brett, indicating they were ready to move.

Brett raised his hand and gave the door three hard raps. They waited for a few moments, but didn't hear anything more. He knocked again, and this time called out, "Police. Open the door."

When there was no answer again, Vanessa looked between them.

"Now what?"

Carter called the chief again. "There is no answer at the door. I want to enter the house without a warrant. We have a missing girl, and we know this perp has used violence before. There is precedent to believe both Martin and Barbara's lives are at risk."

"Proceed with caution. Do you have any reason to suppose Martin himself is armed and dangerous?"

"No, ma'am."

She gave them the go-ahead. Carter reached out and opened the screen door. The back door was cracked open. He pushed it wide and they entered the house together. He wasn't comfortable having Vanessa with them for this, but he and Brett had already discussed that she'd be in more danger waiting in the vehicle.

Room by room, they searched the small house. There was no sign of Martin, although there was evidence that he'd been there recently. There was a plate with breadcrumbs on the counter and the woodburning stove had red-hot coals in it.

"Let's check the barn," Carter suggested to Brett. "I'll take the lead, if you bring up the rear."

They'd keep Vanessa between them. With an armed guard bookending her, she'd be protected.

Both Carter and Brett held their weapons, keeping the barrels pointed at the ground. They silently gravitated toward the barn. Carter saw a buggy with a chestnut horse with white socks hitched up. Apparently, Martin was planning on leaving. He pointed to the buggy. Brett gave him a thumbs-up.

Vanessa caught her breath softly, but made no other outward sign of the tension rife in the air.

The small group flattened themselves against the outer wall of the barn and worked their way toward the open doors. At a signal from Carter, they stopped to listen.

At first, he heard nothing. Then a low groan came from inside. Carter tightened his grip on his gun and breached the entrance. A pair of dark trouser-clad legs on the dirt floor stuck out from the first stall. Carter moved toward them. A second groan echoed ahead.

Carter motioned for Brett and Vanessa to wait. He slid

into the barn and stood still, scanning the open space for any dangers. The only place a killer could ambush them was the single stall that had been built in along the left side of the wall. He backed out of the structure.

"We're clear," he told his companions. Then he returned and carefully made his way to the stall. He looked inside it and sighed before he holstered his weapon. When Brett and Vanessa came toward him, he waved Vanessa closer.

"I need your medical training. I think he's been shot."

Vanessa turned to Brett and asked him to grab the first-aid kit from the cruiser. She approached the man lying on the ground.

"Martin, I'm a nurse. Can I help you?"

"Jah."

Carter marveled at her kindness. This man had drugged her and taken her from the safety of her room and she was treating him with compassion.

Martin needed more than compassion, though. He needed to get to the hospital if he was going to survive his injuries. He called the chief.

"I found Martin. He's been shot. He's alive but looks like he's in bad shape."

Brett returned and handed Vanesa the first-aid kit. She immediately went to work, peeling back his layered clothing to check his wound. Then she began to treat it. "It's still bleeding pretty badly. I need to focus on that. I don't want to move him around too much."

"Is the bullet still in him?" Brett asked.

"I have no way of knowing that. I don't see an exit wound. Given the placement of the wound, if there is an exit, it would be on his back."

Her expression said she hoped there wasn't another hole on his back. That would be two wounds he was bleeding from.

"I'm sending an ambulance and backup to your location."

He examined the young man's ashen complexion. "I hope the ambulance gets here in time."

He had his doubts. Martin's eyes flickered open.

"Barbara?" he said weakly. "Did you find my Barbara?"

Carter eased down beside the wounded man who was bleeding into the hay-strewn ground. "We're looking for her, Martin. Why did you abduct Vanessa Hall this morning?"

Martin coughed and moaned in pain. "He said he'd shoot Barbara."

"Weren't you concerned he'd kill Vanessa in her place?" Brett demanded, his tone nowhere near as calm as Carter's had been.

"He promised she'd be safe. He needed her medical knowledge."

Every word came slower.

"Who said she'd be safe, Martin?" But the man didn't respond. He'd lost consciousness. If that ambulance didn't arrive soon, he'd die.

While Carter felt bad for the young man, urgency pounded through his system. Martin might be the only one who could identify the man responsible for all the terror and chaos of the past several days.

Lives were on the line, and they were running out of time.

FIFTEEN

Vanessa only half listened to Carter's conversation with the chief. The bulk of her attention remained focused on her patient. He seemed to be fading in and out of consciousness. Blood splotches stained both her new denim blue jeans and her sweatshirt. She shrugged. Clothing could be replaced.

Although she'd never wear either of these items again.

Martin's pain-glazed eyes opened again. He blinked up at her, his face contorted in a grimace.

"I'm sorry."

Her normal response—*it's fine*—wouldn't work in this situation. Because it wasn't fine. She understood he feared for his girlfriend, but he'd put another in danger in her place. At the same time, Vanessa had already forgiven him.

"Thank you," she said. "I'm sorry that someone kidnapped Barbara."

She hated to think of what the young woman was enduring.

"Do you know why he took her?" Carter crouched down on the other side, next to Brett.

Martin groaned. "*Jah.* I know. A few months ago, I had surgery on my shoulder. Before the surgery, I was nervous. I talked too much. I talked about Barbara. Our plans to marry soon."

He licked his lips. "Please, can I have some water?"

Brett handed Vanessa the water bottle he'd brought from the car. She shook her head. "I'm sorry. You can't have water until later. You'll need surgery again."

"That's what started my problems. I told him that I didn't want to marry Barbara yet because I'd lost everything in a fire before I moved here. I didn't have enough to offer her yet. A man should provide his wife and *kinder* with a *gut* home. I had forgotten about this conversation until yesterday. He came to my *haus*. He said he had Barbara and would hurt her if I didn't do what he said."

Martin closed his eyes again. Vanessa called his name three times before he responded.

"Martin," Carter said, leaning closer. "What did he tell you to do?"

"He tried to give me a gun. I refused. When I told him I wouldn't hurt anyone, he got angry, but said he had a different plan. He gave me three needles. The kind we use to give shots to our horses. He said he knew where you were." Martin turned his head and spoke directly to her. "I was to get you and bring you to him at his *haus*. Then he'd let my Barbara go. I told him I couldn't hurt anyone. But he promised me that you wouldn't be hurt. You would help him then he'd let you go."

Surely, he couldn't have believed that? A man who'd tried to give him a gun would just let her walk away?

However, it was there in Martin's face. He may not have completely bought the story, but in his desperation, he chose to hope it was the truth. Pity stirred in her soul, edging aside the burning anger, although it didn't abate it. She was furious that someone felt they had the right to treat others this way. To manipulate, coerce and kill others for monetary gain. She had never understood such greed.

"Martin," Carter barked.

The injured man roused himself once more.

"Who was the man? What was his name?"

She held her breath.

"I don't remember."

She clenched her teeth to hold in a scream. They were so close!

"It's on the papers in the *haus*. There's a folder from the hospital somewhere in the kitchen."

Vanessa wanted to run into the house and find the folder. But she couldn't leave her patient.

"I'll go search for the folder." Brett stood and dusted off his uniform. "You two stay here with Martin and wait for the ambulance."

Vanessa didn't want to wait. She wanted her hands on that folder herself. But she nodded.

When Brett walked away, she shot a look at Carter. "You know what this means, right? The ringleader is someone who I work with. A *doctor*! Someone committed to saving lives."

The hypocrisy slammed into her.

Whoever it was, she wanted him to lose more than the license he'd betrayed. She wanted that man to spend his life behind bars.

Carter sat back, shocked by what Martin had admitted. He'd strongly suspected Mandy's killer worked in the medical system. The knowledge that it was a doctor, though... well that floored him.

Vanessa's anger at the betrayal was almost tangible. She vibrated with her fury, and her blue eyes snapped and sparkled.

He didn't blame her. If someone he worked with had betrayed their badge, he'd want to lead the charge to throw them in prison himself.

"I have to call the chief."

She nodded, her jaw still tight. He wanted to lean over and give her a bear hug to show his support but settled for patting her on the shoulder. To his surprise, she grabbed the hand he placed there and squeezed it.

He didn't move away. Just waited, giving her the time she needed. When she released him, he stood and moved out of the stall to use his shoulder radio and check in with his boss.

"The ambulance should be there soon. So should your backup. I'm on my way to talk with Roberts. He's awake and feeling grouchy, or so I've been told."

Carter chuckled, relieved to hear his colleague was on the mend.

"Oh, and I had a Doctor Zachary Hall call me this morning, all fired up because his sister is missing and all his calls aren't going through."

"Ah, yes. Vanessa's phone was destroyed in the fire."

"Well, he heard we had her, so please have her call in and check with her family."

"Will do."

He walked over to Vanessa. Crystalline tears trembled on her long lashes. She'd obviously heard their radio conversation. "You can use my phone and call him."

She laughed shakily. "It's a good thing I know his phone number—and most of my family."

He smiled and handed her his device. "Take your time."

She dialed and put it on speaker.

"Hello, this is Dr. Hall."

A happy grin formed on her lips. It sparked the now familiar yearning for what he couldn't have in his chest, but he didn't look away. They were closing in on the killer. Soon, she'd go back to her life. He had to treasure her presence while he had her with him.

"Zach, it's me. Nessa."

Nessa? He'd not heard her called that before. No, to him she'd always be Vanessa.

"Nessa! Are you alright? I've been worried sick. So have Lillian, Sebastian, Logan and Tanner. We haven't called Mom and Dad yet because the police chief said you were okay. Whose phone is this, anyway?"

"Hold on. Take a breath," she told him, rolling her eyes. "I'm on Lieutenant Carter Flint's phone. I have it on speaker, by the way."

"Why are you on his phone? Where's yours? And what happened to your house? I didn't hear anything about the fire until my rounds in Sterling Ridge yesterday. Someone asked me about my sister. And I had to say I didn't know anything!"

Carter winced at the fury in the other man's voice. He had to admit, he'd be ready to commit mayhem if someone disappeared with his mom. A man liked to know his family was safe.

"I'm sorry. Let me explain." Vanessa ran a hand through her hair. She told him about the fire and about the loss of her phone. "Someone started the fire. The police are close to catching him, and they're keeping me safe."

He raised his eyebrows. She was leaving out large portions about what happened. Her brother raged a bit more, then calmed down. "I'm glad you're okay. Keep us informed, please."

She swallowed. "I will. I've been thinking I need to get better about making time for my family. I love you."

There was a moment of silence. When Zach spoke, his voice was thick with emotion. "We love you, too, baby sister. I'm glad you're coming back to us."

Vanessa handed Carter the phone again with a soft expression on her face. He couldn't help it. He leaned in and kissed her softly. A quick peck, which was barely there and then gone. Her eyes flared wide and she raised her hands to her lips.

His radio beeped, interrupting the moment.

"Yes, Chief?" he said, never taking his gaze off the woman who held his heart.

"Lieutenant Flint, I have big news. I just finished talking with Sergeant Roberts. He said that he thinks he was shot because he saw the man who'd set fire to the house. He'd heard the call and was on the on the way to the house when he nearly ran the man over, still carrying a gas can."

Carter flashed a glance at Vanessa. Her lips twisted in a silent snarl. She looked like a shark that had scented blood in the water. The door slammed and Brett came running into the garage, a file in his hands.

"Who was it, Chief?"

"The anesthesiologist," Brett said.

At the exact same moment, Chief Kaiser said, "Dr. George Findley."

"Of course!" Vanessa snarled.

Carter lifted his eyebrows at her, wondering what she meant. "Did he seem like someone who would commit murder?"

She waved like she was flicking away an insect. "I didn't mean that. He was very polite and polished. But he always seemed a little aloof. No, I said of course, because the voice I heard had the lightest touch of a New York accent. Most of the time, I don't notice it when Dr. Findley speaks, but if he gets excited about something, then it becomes more noticeable. That's probably why I had so much trouble placing it at first."

He nodded. "It makes sense. He was on scene when Mandy was shot. He would have had time to leave the building and circle around."

"Not to mention, the word at the clinic is that he used to be really enthusiastic about target shooting. Although I haven't heard of him doing that in a year or two."

"Chief?" Carter said.

"I'm calling all available units to look for him. And sending a team to his house. He called in sick to work today and yesterday."

"Sure he did," Vanessa muttered darkly. "He's been busy the last couple of days."

He would have smiled if the situation hadn't been so dire.

"We'll wait here until the ambulance crew arrives. After we finish at the scene, we'll head in and join the team."

"Sounds good. Don't take any chances. He's on the loose, and you know he was in that area this morning. He's to be considered armed and dangerous."

"Understood."

Carter and Brett both checked their weapons, their eyes constantly scanning the area. "We're safer in here," Carter told Vanessa. "If we go outside, we'll make ourselves open targets."

What he didn't tell her was that he and Brett would both need to leave the barn once the ambulance arrived to protect the paramedics. The minutes ticked by, each one feeling longer than the one before.

Finally, Vanessa raised her head. "I hear an ambulance siren."

Brett and Carter both moved to the door. When Vanessa moved toward them, Carter asked her to remain with Martin. She glared but did as he asked.

He understood why. It was hard to remain in place when

answers were within reach. The danger hadn't passed, though, and he would do his best to keep his promise to get her safely back to her family.

Within a minute, the ambulance arrived. Tires crunched on the gravel driveway outside the barn. The paramedics turned off the siren and the lights and hopped out of the ambulance. Brett and Carter escorted them into the barn.

"Vanessa!" Sydney called. "I'm happy to see you are still in one piece."

"Thanks. This is Martin." Vanessa indicated the man. He'd once again lapsed into unconsciousness. "I tended his wound the best I could."

The paramedics took his vitals. Both of their countenances flattened. Martin was in serious condition. They lifted him on a gurney and rolled him to the ambulance. Carter and Brett provided cover while they loaded the patient up and drove away.

"Okay. Let's finish here and get back to town," Carter said, taking out his phone.

A shot broke the peace.

Carter stumbled forward, his back burning.

"Carter!"

He fell backward. His head bounced off a rock.

SIXTEEN

Carter tried to sit up, but hands held him down.

"Careful, buddy. You've been shot," Brett said.

He knew that. But that wasn't his worry right now. "Vanessa?"

Brett hesitated.

"Brett, where's Vanessa?"

"I don't know."

Carter pinned his friend with a glare, only then noticing that Brett's shoulder was wounded. "He shot you, too."

"We were ambushed. I didn't lose consciousness. But he got me in the shoulder and the leg."

Carter's gaze dropped to the bandaged area on Brett's shin. Brett wasn't standing, but it didn't look like anything was broken. "Can you stand?"

"Yeah. After you were shot, I returned fire. He got me in the leg. I fell. But I managed to get back on my feet. I heard Vanessa yell out Findley's name. By the time I reached them, he forced her into his car and shot at me again. This time he hit my shoulder."

"I assume you called it in?" Carter would never know how he managed to speak so calmly in those minutes. Blood pounded in his ears. Vanessa was in the clutches of a cold-blooded murderer. The man didn't want her dead, he reminded himself.

Not yet.

Carter felt like ice was slushing in his veins. How long did she have before he decided she was of no use to him anymore?

Stop. He couldn't let his mind go there. He needed to remain focused on what needed to be done if he wanted to get her back alive.

He didn't want to think about going on without her in his world. She brought color and light to it just by breathing. He loved her. He loved her laugh, her sassiness and the mile-long stubborn streak she often displayed. He loved her compassion and her strength in dealing with life's struggles, both her own traumas and those of others.

He would find her, no matter how long it took, or what he personally sacrificed. He would bring her home.

Another ambulance pulled into the yard, followed a few minutes later by another cruiser. Carter blinked when Chief Kaiser herself exited.

"Chief." He forced himself to stand then reached down to give Brett a hand up.

She looked between them. "Do you men need to be relieved from duty?"

"No," they both responded.

"Let us look them over before they make that decision," the first paramedic said.

Carter sat while she took his vitals and treated his wound, his leg jiggling with impatience. He needed to rescue Vanessa. With every second, she got farther away from them.

"You're good," the paramedic finally announced. "The bullet barely grazed you. I expect you were knocked out because you bumped your head when you fell. Your pupils look fine. You should come to the hospital and have yourself checked out."

"I will when this is done," he promised.

She gave him a disapproving glance. He ignored it. It was the best he could do.

Once she headed over to help with Brett, the chief came closer.

"The team went over to Findley's house. He wasn't there, nor had he been there for a few days, it looked like."

"Martin said Findley told him to meet at his house."

"We are looking into other properties he might own. Or that his ex-wife might have owned. Trust me, we haven't given up."

The paramedics were both frustrated when Brett also refused to go to the hospital. "Why call us if you won't let us take care of you?"

"We thank you," the chief assured them. "We have three lives at stake right now, though. I will personally see that they go to the hospital as soon as the crisis is over."

The paramedics grumbled all the way to their ambulance. Once they were inside, Carter and Brett both rounded on the chief.

"Three lives?" Carter demanded. "Vanessa and Barbara are the only two I know about. Or were you referring to Martin?"

She shook her head. "Unfortunately, no."

"Who else?" Brett's face was stony. "Who else is in danger?"

"I got a phone call about an hour ago from a precinct an hour and half west of here. They had an Amish man call them and report that his wife, who is nearly at her due date, went to an appointment at the local medical clinic. He dropped her off and then went to run some errands in town. When he returned two hours later, his wife was gone. Someone recalled seeing her get into a dark sedan."

Carter exchanged a glance with Brett.

"He took Vanessa in a car like that," Brett confirmed.

"When?" Carter demanded. "When did the woman disappear?"

"Two days ago."

About the time that Findley started trying to kidnap Vanessa.

"Martin claimed that Findley needed Vanessa's medical expertise."

"That's weak. He's a doctor," Brett scoffed.

Carter thought for a moment. "He is, but he's an anesthesiologist. Not an obstetrician or a midwife. Not even a surgeon. He might need a specific kind of help."

"He wants the baby delivered now."

Both men stared at their chief, horrified at the implication. Because either forcing a labor or any other procedure would be heinous. And after that, would all three women's lives be forfeited?

Vanessa had fought against Dr. Findley's punishing grasp as he'd wrapped the coarse rope around her wrists. She had felt the tiny bones scraping together under her skin. Once he had the rope securely knotted, her discomfort didn't let up. Instead of his crushing hold, the scratchy rope rubbed her tender flesh raw.

He had the advantage of strength. In addition, he'd forced her onto the back floorboard, where she sat wedged between the back seat and the front passenger seat. There was nowhere for her to go to escape.

"Don't fight so hard," he had warned her, his voice almost pleasant. He had shoved her legs deeper into the back of his car. "I'm an outdoorsman. I know how to tie a solid knot. You won't be able to get free."

"Why are you doing this?" she asked as he drove.

He shrugged. "I need the money. You have no idea the ludicrous extremes some people will go through, or the amount of money they will spend, for a baby."

She swallowed, appalled.

"You swore an oath to do no harm."

He snickered. "You're so pathetic. Please. I'm not harming these babies. They're going to good homes. After all, anyone who can afford to pay sixty thousand dollars, cash, for a baby can afford to buy the brats anything."

"But what about their mothers?"

He shrugged. "They aren't hurt. Most of them."

It was the *most* that made her nearly retch. Plus, the fact that he seemed to feel ripping families to shreds wasn't harm made her head spin.

"I thought about older children. They're easier to get. But the market wasn't there. People want newborns, so that's what I gave them."

She didn't want to hear anything more. Every word made her sicker at heart.

"You seemed really shocked to see me. Didn't you know it was me? I thought you'd figure it out before now."

She couldn't answer. No, she hadn't figured it out, but now, listening to him, she could picture him talking to Mandy on the phone. Another thought occurred to her.

"Did Mandy know?"

He scoffed. "I wasn't born yesterday. I knew from the beginning I needed to find helpers that were desperate enough to do anything for a stranger." He paused. "It helped that none of them were indispensable."

Dispensable was how he'd described Mandy, the woman he'd killed because she made a mistake. Vanessa shuddered.

Thankfully, Dr. Findley subsided into a smug silence. There wasn't a hint of shame or regret about him. He reached out and turned a dial, although she couldn't tell which one. What she could see was how his hand trembled.

But it wasn't fear.

"Hmm." The car swayed. He'd turned a corner. "We're almost there. Just another ten minutes."

By the time he'd stopped the vehicle, Vanessa's long legs were cramped from being folded up in such an uncomfortable position for so long. She felt like a pretzel. He disappeared from view only to pop back up like a weasel when he opened the door and dragged her out.

Pain shot up her legs. She nearly collapsed. He wouldn't let her. He forced her to march toward the small house with a long driveway and no garage. To her disappointment, there were no houses on either side. No one would hear her if she screamed for help.

Dr. Findley looked at her face and laughed. "Silly Vanessa, did you really think I'd walk you around like this if there were neighbors close by? This house belonged to my late ex-wife. No one comes here anymore. I bought it from her estate nearly three years ago for hunting, but, of course, I can't hunt anymore."

He held up a shaking hand.

She was afraid to ask what happened. And then he opened the door and a new horror met her eyes.

Inside the house, a young Amish woman quivered in one corner, her face bruised. "That one thought she'd escape," he said.

Then she noticed that she was chained to a wall. As if she was an animal on exhibit at a zoo. Disgust welled up in her. But she knew better than to fight. She wasn't the only one in danger here.

Then a chair creaked on the other side of the room.

Vanessa whipped her head toward the sound. Her jaw dropped. An Amish woman in her mid-twenties stood, her hands curved protectively over her stomach. Under her apron, she was clearly close to the end of her third trimester.

Vanessa didn't recognize the woman. She wasn't someone who had ever visited the clinic.

It hit her. It wouldn't have mattered how many homes she and Carter had visited. This woman wasn't on the list they had compiled.

Thinking of Carter made her heart hurt. She'd seen his body on the ground when Dr. Findley had dragged her to his car. Had he survived? She had just started to make connections with her family. And she had fallen in love with a wonderful man.

But one man had separated her from both.

Neither woman reacted to her presence other than to peer at the rope around her wrists.

What did he want with her?

"Now that you are all here, we can begin." He whirled and faced Vanessa. "I need a baby. Now. The contract has been made and paid for. You are going to help me."

She started to shake her head. "I don't know how you think I can help you."

She bit her lip. She should have kept silent. She didn't want to provoke him to say anything else. One of the women, she couldn't tell which one, whispered something in Pennsylvania Dutch. Their captor whirled to face them.

Vanessa noticed the door remained open. She instinctively backed toward the door while his back faced her. She could run and get help. It was foolish, she knew that, but she was the only one capable of trying to escape. If she didn't try, they had little hope of extricating themselves from this mess.

Unless Carter was alive. He'd keep looking. Would he find her?

She silently prayed for his safety and for rescue.

Then she took another step back. Her foot landed on the small front porch. The boards under her feet creaked.

Dr. Findley whipped around and had her wrists in a bruising grip before she could take another step.

"Oh, no, you don't. You are not going anywhere. I didn't spend the past two days trying to get you here to let you escape me. You're too important right now. I need you to help me get this baby."

She stared at him, all her hope fading away. "I don't know what you want me to do. There's nothing to be done."

Whatever he had in mind, she knew it wouldn't be ethical or safe for any of them.

"Yes, there is." He leaned in and lowered his voice. The very softness of his tone made him seem all the more menacing. "You're a midwife. You are going to help me perform an emergency caesarean section."

She stared at him, her entire body shaking.

She'd fallen into the worst nightmare of her life.

SEVENTEEN

Vanessa's heart pounded in her chest. She stared at him. "You want me to do what?"

He yanked her deeper inside the room and kicked the door with his heel. It swung partially closed. The younger woman whimpered. The other woman left her seat and made her way painfully to her companion's side.

Both women's faces said they were staring at their own deaths and they knew it.

"Her!" He pointed a shaky finger at the pregnant woman. "I need her baby. I have clients waiting for a newborn. They've already paid for it! But because of you, I have no baby to give them. Do you have any idea what you've cost me?"

Vanessa held herself still, desperate to still the tremble running up and down her spine, as he turned the gun in his left hand on her.

"But I can't. I'm not a doctor. I'm only a midwife. I have assisted in C-sections, but I don't know how to do one."

He sneered. "Please, I've assisted in them, too. In fact, I've done it so many times, I think I could do the procedure myself, if my hands didn't shake so much."

And they were. The gun in his hand wobbled as if he'd drop it at any moment. Suddenly it made sense. Dr. Findley used to be an avid hunter. The other hospital staff would joke about how he'd bring in three or four deer every year. Not only that, but he and a buddy also belonged to a sportsman club. They'd go there weekly to shoot targets. Dr. Findley always won. Until he'd been in a skiing accident and needed surgery. It had been a tough recovery.

After that, he'd given up shooting for sport.

Rumor had it that he had become addicted to the narcotics prescribed for pain. However, she hadn't known if the rumor was true. She'd seen no signs of addiction. In fact, she'd dismissed the claims. But now, it seemed his addiction was indeed why he couldn't shoot a moving target. That was why she was still alive.

Unless she refused his request.

But she couldn't perform a C-section on a woman just to save her own life. In her mind, she whispered a prayer for delivery. And if not for her, then a prayer for the safety of these two women, both innocent victims of one man's greed.

Backing away from her colleague, she shook her head. "No. I won't do it."

"If you don't, the other girl will die. I've already killed her boyfriend. After so many deaths, one more won't bother me."

A wounded cry filled the room. The young girl—who was probably Barbara—sobbed, and sank to the floor.

She must not know that Martin had survived. How could she, trapped here in this place?

"He's alive, Barbara." Vanessa kept her attention trained on Findley while she reassured the young woman. "He was injured, but he was alive."

Findley snarled. "I can still kill her."

It was only a matter of time. Vanessa knew there was not much she could do to stop him if he decided to kill all of them. Even though there were three of them, only one of them would fight. Amish were pacifists and would never use violence, even to protect themselves or their families. She would fight, but Findley had the advantages of strength and training on his side.

And he had a gun. At this close range, she wouldn't pose any challenge. Trapped within these walls, she wouldn't be able to move far enough away to escape.

If she could get the weapon away from him, she might be able to defend herself. But how would she manage that? He was bigger and stronger. The only possibility would be if she could distract him.

"Don't even try it," he said calmly. "I've already wasted too much time on you. The only reason you're alive is because I need you."

He looked pointedly at the other two occupants in the room.

She understood. If she refused to help, she was no use and he had no qualms about killing her. Or anyone else.

Over his shoulder, she had a clear view out the window. In the trees, two figures skulked closer. She didn't know how she knew, but she was positive Carter was the person in the lead. He'd found her. She only needed to remain alive for the next few minutes. Just long enough for help to arrive.

Switching her gaze back to George Findley, she tried to keep her expression from giving away her renewed hope and excitement.

"If I help, do you promise you'll let both of them live?"

He smirked. "Sure, I can do that."

It was a lie. She knew it and Dr. Findley did, too. He didn't plan on letting any of them leave this place once he had what he wanted from her.

Behind her, one of the women began weeping. The sound broke her heart. Vanessa stiffened her spine and did her best to ignore the crying. If her ploy worked, this nightmare would soon be over and they would all be on their way home.

If it didn't work, they'd all be dead within moments.

"Ok, let me think. I don't recall how to begin the surgery."

"I don't believe you," Findley snarled, raising his gun again. "You're stalling for time. It won't work."

Vanessa swallowed, tasting bile. She'd failed.

Saying a quick prayer for the women and unborn child behind her, she braced herself, preparing to use her own body as a shield.

Glancing at the window, her eyes met Carter's. Her breath caught.

He raised his gun toward Findley.

"Down!" she yelled at the women, throwing her body to the side.

Carter shot through the window. Glass shattered, and small shards hit the flood and skittered. Findley cried out, dropping the gun, his hand bloody. With an angry curse, he fled the room.

Brett shouted. His feet pounded after the fleeing doctor.

Carter burst into the cabin. Seeing him, Vanessa flung herself into his arms and let the fear flow out in a stream of tears.

She was alive. They all were.

Carter tightened his arms around Vanessa and buried his nose in her hair, inhaling the spicy scent that he would forever associate with the woman he loved.

He no longer doubted his own heart. He held everything he wanted for his future against his chest. His pulse filled his ears. For a moment, he just breathed.

But he had a job to do. After giving Vanessa one final squeeze, he dropped his arms and stepped away from her, then turned to look at the two women huddled together in the corner of the room.

He spoke softly. "Barbara? And Priscilla?"

They nodded. Barbara straightened, but Priscilla remained crouched, her arms wrapped protectively around her belly. When she groaned and scrunched her face into a pained grimace, his blood froze.

"Priscilla?" Vanessa moved around him, completely focused on the pregnant woman, looking every inch a professional midwife, even with the dirt and a bruise forming on her cheek. "How long have you been having contractions?"

"For the past two hours. They weren't bad at first." She paused as another contraction struck. When the pain dwindled from her face, she began to speak again. "I didn't want to say anything because I didn't want that man to know my *boppli* was coming. I was scared. Scared that he would have killed you," she said to Vanessa.

Carter felt himself turn pale. Both because he realized how close Vanessa had come to death, and because he might have to help deliver a baby. He had been trained in first aid. Theoretically, he knew what to do in such a situation. But he had never assisted a woman in childbirth. He had zero experience.

He hovered near Vanessa's elbow for a couple of minutes while she questioned Priscilla in case she needed his help. Once it was clear she had everything under control, he called the chief.

"Lieutenant. What do you have for me?"

He turned away from the women and stood between them and the door. Both to give them privacy and so he'd intercept any threats. He continuously scanned the windows to ensure danger didn't catch them unawares.

"Chief, Dr. Findley has fled the scene. Lieutenant Talbot

is in pursuit. I am in the cabin with Nurse Hall and the two abducted women. They are all alive."

"I'm rerouting all units to your location. What is their condition, Lieutenant? Do you require an ambulance?"

"Yes, ma'am. Priscilla Lapp is in labor."

The chief was silent for a few moments after he dropped that bit of news on her.

"She's having the baby, right now!" Vanessa called out. Her voice remained steady, but it throbbed with urgency.

As if to echo her statement, Priscilla screamed in agony.

Carter nearly dropped the phone. He had always heard labor took hours. Sometimes a whole day or more.

Carter quickly disconnected with the chief and said, "What do I do?"

"Come here!"

He kneeled near Vanessa. She had made Priscilla as comfortable as possible on the floor. The next thirty minutes were grueling. About halfway through, Brett came to the door and knocked. Carter left the women and went outside, leaving the door ajar so he'd hear any disturbance.

"Did you find him?"

"No, sorry. I'm not giving up, though. They rest of the units have started arriving."

"That's good. I'm assuming you'll continue searching now that you have backup."

"Of course. We'll be launching a full-scale search for the doctor as soon as we get organized."

"I'll stay here to guard the women," Carter announced.

There was no way he'd leave them, not now. Someone had to protect the women. Carter was concerned about all of them. But mostly Vanessa.

Within five minutes, the area was filled with officers of

various ranks and years of experience. He even noticed a couple of firefighters had joined in. The more help, the better.

Brett and his other colleagues spread out and organized into a parallel search pattern, one best suited for large outdoor areas. He went back inside, the sound of Brett's orders ringing in his ears.

Carter closed the door and returned to Vanessa's side just in time to see her wrapping a small baby in Priscilla's cloak. The child's cry brought a sting to his own eyes.

This case had the potential to end in tragedy, Instead, lives had been saved and a new one had been nurtured into the world.

Vanessa handed Priscilla her baby. "She seems healthy. Good reflexes and a strong set of lungs."

Carter chuckled. Barbara covered her smiling mouth behind her hands and giggled.

"Danke." Tears ran down Priscilla's cheeks. She stroked her baby girl's face.

"The ambulance will be here soon," Carter told them. "At the hospital, they'll give the baby a thorough checkup. And you, also."

"Will I get to see Martin?" Barbara asked.

Carter hesitated. He'd been involved in a kidnapping and an assault. His fate had yet to be decided. "Maybe. He was severely injured. I don't know if they are allowing visitors yet."

When the ambulance pulled in front of the house, Vanessa stood next to Carter while the paramedics took care of Priscilla, the baby and Barbara.

Vanessa swayed on her feet. Without considering how it would look to witnesses, Carter hooked an arm around her waist and looped her in closer so she leaned against him.

Vanessa sighed and nestled her head on his shoulder. He gave in to the urge to kiss the top of her red hair. He smiled when Priscilla's baby began to cry from the back of the ambulance. It was a glorious sound.

Shouts came from the rear of the house, followed by pounding feet.

Dr. George Findley burst into the clearing, his eyes wild behind his thick-framed glasses. The ambulance doors slammed closed, shutting the infant's wails inside.

"No!"

The howl coming from the dignified doctor's throat made the hair stand up on Carter's arms. Carter moved to block the path to the ambulance. But then, the doctor shifted directions and raced at Vanessa.

He slipped a hand under his jacket and pulled out a gun. Even while he ran, he aimed and shot. Brett shot at the same time. The doctor toppled over and landed face down on the snow.

Brett and another officer were on him in seconds. "He's alive. But barely."

Carter ran to Vanessa. She staggered toward him, blood pouring down the side of her face. "Carter?"

She fell forward. He caught her in his arms. "Vanessa!"

She didn't respond. Blood stained his coat. He didn't care. His world had shrunk to the woman lying unconscious in his embrace. Dimly aware of Brett on the phone with Dispatch, Carter picked Vanessa up and carried her into the cabin. At least there, he could set her somewhere dry. Gently, he placed her on the floor, as if she was fine porcelain he was afraid would break.

Her head wound was the only injury he found. A new paramedic ran into the cabin. A second ambulance must have arrived.

Together, they worked to stem the bleeding. Carter was

grateful that the woman didn't chatter at him. He didn't think himself capable of holding a coherent conversation.

After what felt like forever, a second paramedic arrived in the room. Carter reluctantly backed off so they could lift her onto a stretcher and remove her from the cabin to the waiting ambulance.

Carter stared after the vehicle when it departed, sirens wailing and lights flashing.

"You okay, buddy?"

He shook his head at Brett. "How did we not prevent that? We have two people on the way to the hospital that should not be there at all. What were we thinking?"

"I get it. But we did our best to capture Findley."

Something in his tone made Carter turn. He narrowed his eyes. "What?"

Brett rubbed the back of his neck. "They don't think Findley will survive."

Carter sighed. Death on their watch was never something they celebrated. "I really wanted to see him serve time for his crimes."

"Me, too. Come on, I'll drive. We'll stop by Good Samaritan Hospital."

Carter didn't argue. He usually drove, but didn't have it in him at the moment. Every mile closer to the hospital, the more anxious he grew. His foot tapped furiously on the floorboard. He caught Brett looking at it a time or two, and tried to still his movements, but a minute later, they started again.

"I'll drop you off and park."

When Brett pulled under the carport, Carter leaped from the vehicle and speedwalked into the hospital. The girl behind the front desk looked at him, smiling. "May I help you?"

He cleared his throat. "I'm Lieutenant Carter Flint. A

young woman was brought in with a gunshot wound. Vanessa Hall—"

"Oh!" The girl's eyes widened. "Vanessa was shot! I just got here. Hold on."

Carter winced at his own thoughtlessness. Of course, Vanessa would be known to some of the people employed at the main hospital. She was a nurse, even if most of her time was spent at the clinic.

Her hands shook as she tapped on the computer keypad. "She's been rushed to the emergency room," the receptionist told him. "Her family has been contacted and are on their way in. You can wait in the waiting area until we have more information."

The moment he walked away from the desk, she disappeared, no doubt to compose herself.

An hour later, he was still there waiting. The doors whooshed open and a tall man with military-short bright red hair and wire-rimmed glasses strode in, looking like he was ready for a fight. He had to be one of Vanessa's brothers. But which one? Clinging to his arm was a shorter brunette who looked like she could have been on TV.

The magnetic couple went straight to the front desk. "I'm Special Agent Tanner Hall. I got a call that my sister is here."

Tanner and Fran. Vanessa's oldest brother and his wife. Vanessa had said she had two brothers in law enforcement. He didn't recall her ever saying one of them was in the FBI.

Carter stepped forward. "Agent Hall?"

Tanner swung around, worry glinting in his eyes. "Yes?"

"I'm Lieutenant Carter Flint." He wasn't sure what else to say. "Can we talk for a few moments? The doctor hasn't come out yet."

Tanner exchanged glances with his wife before agreeing. Carter sat with them in the chairs farthest from any of the families and explained about Dr. Findley and how he had targeted Vanessa. He told them about the kidnapping and the rescue.

He didn't tell them that he was in love with Vanessa. She needed to hear it first. By the time he finished, tears were rolling down Fran's face and Tanner's complexion was ashen.

He answered as many of their questions as he could.

"What about this Dr. Findley?" Tanner growled.

"He didn't survive."

Tanner scowled, obviously no more happy with that update than Carter had been.

"Hall family?" A doctor stood in the doorway. Tanner and Fran stepped forward to speak with the surgeon. Carter stayed long enough to hear "in a coma."

He choked down his emotion. He wanted to stay, to see her for himself. But he couldn't. Her family had that right, not him. He slipped past Vanessa's family. The word *coma* bothered him. How long would that last? He departed, praying with all his might that Vanessa would come out of the coma and make a full recovery.

If she did, would she want him by her side?

Because he didn't know if he could go back to a dull life that didn't include her vibrant presence.

EIGHTEEN

"Dude, what's up with you?" Brett tossed his empty Pepsi can toward the blue recycle bin against the wall, giving a mock cheer when it hit the side and dropped in.

"I don't know what you mean." His conscience twinged at the fib. Carter knew exactly what his friend and partner referred to, but he didn't want to talk about his near-obsessive behavior in the past three days.

"Yeah, you do." Swiveling his chair to face Carter, Brett leaned his forearms on his desk and clasped his hands together.

Carter immediately recognized his we're-here-until-I-get-some-answers pose. He'd seen Brett in that mode too many times to doubt that they'd indeed sit there until either he spilled his guts, which he didn't want to do, or until a call came in. Even then, Brett would only take up the conversation again later.

It was better to get it over with.

Still, he was reluctant to get into a feelings discussion. "Don't worry about it. I'm fine."

Brett scoffed. "Fine? Fine! You've been distracted for the past three days. You constantly look at the clock or your phone. You've never been chatty, but you're worse than ever now. And the moment your shift is done, you're out of here. So I'll ask again. What going on?"

He knew he'd been a bit off, but hearing Brett describing it, he winced. "Sorry, buddy. I guess I didn't realize..."

"Stop. I don't want an apology. I don't care about any of that. Just a bit worried about my best friend, that's all."

Carter sighed. "Vanessa is still in the hospital. I go and visit every evening after work. Well, I try—her brothers and sister have all been around. They take turns. I've met them all now. They let me have a turn, too, but it's not much."

Brett sat far back in his chair. The swivel chair creaked as it reclined. "Not her parents?"

"They're usually there in the morning. They go home in the evening because Mr. Hall needs to check in on his sister in the evening. She fell and broke her hip."

"Her family is there. So she doesn't need you anymore."

"She's still unconscious." Even he heard the agony resonating in his tone.

Brett straightened up so fast, his chair wobbled. "You're in love with her."

Carter opened his mouth to protest. Then snapped it shut. What was the point? "I am. I'm not sure how it happened so fast, but it did. So I go and talk to her, hoping she'll hear me. Not knowing if she cares the same."

"I'm sorry, man. That's the pits."

Carter laughed, shaking his head. "Yeah, it is."

"I don't know anything about being in love. But you know I've got your six."

Carter nodded, acknowledging the military phrase of brotherhood and support. He appreciated it more than he could ever say. For the next hour, the two worked, finishing up reports with a little conversation mixed in.

The moment his shift ended, though, Carter snapped his

laptop closed and stood, snagging his jacket off the back of his chair. Brett watched without comment. Carter sketched a slight wave before striding away from the desk.

He strode down the hall and out into the bright sunlight. For the next six weeks, he was on the seven-to-three shift, so he would be able to see some sunlight. While the landscape looked like a Norman Rockwell painting with the blue sky, fluffy clouds and the pristine snow, accompanied by the Christmas trees and lights lining the main street, he hurried toward his truck, anxious to be out of the weather. He shoved his hands into the pockets of his coat. It must have been twenty degrees or less. What a fine day to leave his gloves in his vehicle. Brett had been right. He'd been so distracted. Carter didn't even recall feeling the cold when he walked into the station earlier in his shift.

One more day. He had to work one more day, and then he'd be off for two.

Please, God, let Vanessa wake up soon. It was only three days until Christmas. She had to be awake for that.

Not that he'd be around. Now that her family was here, and now that she had rediscovered her faith, she might not need him, or want him, by her side.

If that was the case, he'd accept it. For now. At least he'd have the opportunity to see her, and maybe one day, she'd let him be part of her world.

But at least she'd be well.

He shook his head. Enough with all the morbid thoughts. It did no good to dwell on what may or may not happen. All he could control was what he did now.

He made quick work of the fluffy white snow dusting his truck then got inside and headed to the hospital. Once there, he parked and jogged through the parking lot, adrenalin spiking in his blood. Soon, he'd see Vanessa.

Would she open those blue eyes today?

The doctors believed it was only a matter of time. Her brain-activity levels were steady. She was breathing on her own.

Tanner, Vanessa's oldest brother, met him in the lobby.

"Hey, Carter." Tanner held out a hand.

Carter shook hands with the other man. "Tanner. Any changes?"

Tanner shook his head, worry lines tightening around his blue eyes, so like his sister's. "Not yet. But we're hoping. Always hoping and praying."

"I'm with you on that."

"Look, Carter, can you come with me for a minute?"

Curious, Carter nodded. The two men walked into the waiting room. Tanner led him to an older couple. Carter would have known them anywhere. Mr. Hall's red hair had gone completely gray, but his wife's, while faded, was still a lovely shade of red. Both stood when he approached with their son.

Carter was aware of other family members in the room. Sebastian and Logan sat together in a corner, watching, and no doubt, listening. Lillian and Zach must have been in with Vanessa now. The hospital was pretty strict about only two visitors at a time.

Mr. Hall reached out a hand when Tanner introduced him. "We are pleased to have you join us, Lieutenant Flint. My children have told me you visit our Vanessa daily."

He didn't miss the question lingering in the older man's eyes.

"Yes, sir."

"Are you the officer who saved her life?" Mrs. Hall asked in a husky contralto voice.

He could have said yes and left it at that. Especially since so many ears were tuned in. But he wanted to begin as he meant to go on with these people. Which meant complete honesty.

"I am. I'm also the cop who's heart and soul in love with your daughter."

Lots of red eyebrows rose at that statement. Tears filled the woman's eyes.

"Ah! And does Vanessa..."

He shrugged. "I don't know. We've never talked about feelings. It wouldn't have been appropriate, given the circumstances."

"I'm glad she had someone like you with her," Mrs. Hall said. "Please, join us."

He lowered himself to a chair. He sat with the family, listening to stories of Vanessa as a stubborn child. He was warmed, even while his heart ached, missing her.

Half an hour after he arrived, Lillian and Zach entered the waiting room.

"Next," Zach said, his smile tight.

Carter's heart sank. She hadn't woken yet.

Vanessa's mother grabbed his arm and gave it a warm squeeze. "We've all been in to visit her already. Why don't you go sit with Nessa for a few minutes? We'll talk more when you return."

Gratitude welled in his chest. Thanking her, he strode from the waiting room to go and sit next to the woman he loved.

He told her of his day. "I really enjoyed meeting your parents. Your mom looks like an older version of you. They asked if I saved your life. I told them I had. I also told them I loved you. I made your mom cry with that one. Sorry about that. I couldn't say anything when they asked how you felt. We never talked about it, and I don't even know if you're interested in dating anyone, much less a cop who works crazy shifts."

He didn't say anything about his own mother. She couldn't help her disease. And Vanessa had always been compassionate toward those with issues.

A movement broke through his ruminations. Turning his head, he stared into her bright blue eyes.

"Vanessa!" he choked, emotion clogging his throat. He fumbled for her hand. She gripped his fingers.

"I would," she murmured, in a soft, breathy voice.

"Would what?"

"I would definitely date a cop with a crazy work schedule."

Vanessa fought against the exhaustion weighing her down. She had heard Carter's voice, but it took her longer than she liked to focus in on what he said. Had he said he loved her?

She didn't want to ask, just in case she heard wrong. But she needed to know.

"I heard you talking. It was the most beautiful sound I ever heard."

He flushed. "How much did you hear?"

She frowned, wrinkling her brow. "I'm not sure. It felt like I was listening underwater for a while."

As hard as she tried, she couldn't ask what she really wanted to know. Not yet.

Memories started crashing in on her. "How long have I been here? The last thing I recall, Dr. Findley tried to kill me." She swallowed hard. "What happened to him?"

Would he ever come after her again? She'd never forget the hatred in his stare when he attacked her, blaming her for his imminent downfall.

Carter's clasp firmed. "That was three days ago. You've

been in a coma since then. As for the doctor, he never recovered from his wounds, although the surgeons did their best. He's dead."

She blinked back the tears. "I can't believe it. We worked together. I liked him. He tried to kill me. For money!"

"He had a prescription addiction and gambling debts. Nearly quarter of a million dollars' worth."

Her jaw dropped. "What? That's unreal! How could he get that into debt? He's a doctor. Have you seen where he lives?"

"He has a thing for rare cars."

She knew there was more to it than that. "What about all the people helping him?"

"We're pretty sure that he was the leader of the abduction ring. We have made some more arrests. Two of his accomplices were willing to sing to lessen their sentences. They were looking at multiple sentences that no doubt would result in them dying in a cage. We believe they gave us everyone. And," he leaned forward and held her gaze, "we are in the process of recovering all the babies."

She caught her breath. "All of them?"

"Yes. They were sold in Ohio, Indiana and Illinois. We've found them all."

"What about their families?" No matter how this turned out, someone got hurt.

His face hardened. "They all knew they were working with an illegal ring. They'll face time. Believe me."

The sympathy filling her soul bled out. To deliberately take someone else's child? No way would she feel sorry for them. They'd get what they deserved.

And the grieving families would have their children back.

Her eyes were growing heavy again. She forced them to remain open. Her mind flew back to what he'd said. "I've been out for three days?"

"Afraid so. Your entire family is downstairs in the waiting room. We've been taking turns visiting you."

"I heard you say you met my mom and dad." She snuggled into the pillow, unable to find a comfortable spot.

He reached out and took her hand, rubbing his thumb in circular motions on the back of it. She shivered. "I did. I met your whole family. They've been gracious enough to let me visit with you a few times."

How much had he been here?

He started to stand. "I should call them, let them know you're awake."

She gripped his hand, hard. "No. Wait. Once you call them, we won't get a moment alone. We need to talk. Don't we?"

Her cheeks heated at her boldness. But she had to know where they stood. If he didn't return her feelings, she'd avoid him. But if he did...

She let the thought linger. Had she heard him right?

Apparently, he was thinking along the same lines. His ears turned red. "Did you, um, hear what else I said?"

She bit her lip, but kept her eyes locked with his. "I think so, but I'm afraid I might have heard wrong."

There. He has the perfect excuse to change his wording and deny it.

Instead, he leaned closer. "I said I loved you."

Tears finally flooded her eyes and spilled over. "I hoped that's what you said. Oh, Carter, couldn't you see that I'd developed feelings for you, too?"

His eyes lit up and a happy grin split his face. "I thought so, when we kissed, but then you seemed to withdraw. I wondered if I'd pushed you beyond your comfort zone."

She snorted. "It wasn't that. I hadn't been involved with anyone since college. The emotions you fired up in me confused me. Not to mention, I had a lot of baggage I needed to work through. I kind of went into overload mode."

He slowly bent down, stopping when his face hovered six inches above hers. "And now? How do you feel now?"

"Why don't you kiss me and find out?" she whispered. Removing his hand from hers, she placed it on his chest. His strong heartbeat under her palm comforted her. He covered her hand with his and closed the distance between them.

His lips brushed hers once. Then again. His head lifted a fraction. She opened her eyes and smiled, joy rushing through every ending. He smiled and lowered his head again in a sweet lingering kiss, full of promises and hope.

"Hey! That's my sister you're kissing."

Groaning, Vanessa tore her lips from Carter. When she glanced at Tanner, he grinned at her, tears sparkling in his eyes.

"Tanner?"

She had never seen him cry before. Not even when she was a child. It freaked her out.

"Sis." He cleared his throat and shrugged. "Sorry to interrupt. Mom and Dad sent me to see if you wanted to join us for dinner, Carter. I think we might table that, though. Everyone's going to want to see Vanessa again."

He stepped closer to her bed, slapping Carter on the back as he passed him. She'd witnessed such brotherly interactions all her life. It looked like Carter was already welcomed into the family.

Tanner kissed her forehead. "Wait 'til I tell the whole them you're back with us, Bunny! They'll be so happy."

Her mouth dropped open. Of course, he'd bring up that ridiculous nickname now, right when she and Carter were sorting things out. He dashed out of the room and disappeared.

"We only have moments before we're ambushed," she

warned Carter, grimacing. In reality, she was glad to see her family. It might take a while, but she would no longer put up barriers to keep an emotional distance between them.

"Bunny?" He sent her a crooked half smile.

"Yeah, well, you don't get to hear that story yet. Maybe in a year or two."

He laughed. "You can tell me on our first anniversary."

She blushed, her breath catching in her throat. Suddenly, she envisioned their future opening up before her eyes. Carter and her, their families, and maybe, one day, children of their own.

For the first time in years, thoughts of what lie ahead didn't frighten her, and make her feel alone.

She reached for Carter. He took her hand and raised it to his lips. The skin where his lips touched tingled.

No, she wasn't alone. She had God on her side, and He'd blessed her with a second chance at love.

She was going to make it count.

EPILOGUE

A year later

She'd always wanted a Christmas wedding.

Vanessa peered out the window. The limousine she'd rented had seemed so spacious when she'd first checked it out. However, once she and her four bridesmaids were piled inside, it didn't seem quite so roomy.

"I can't believe my baby sister is getting married," Lillian said for the third time, her red braid and porcelain complexion glowing against the green-and-gold, maid-of-honor dress she wore.

"You've said that before," Darlene teased Vanessa's sister.

"Yeah, yeah. I'm just happy."

Vanessa listened to the chatter around her, smiling. Her heart was too full for her to join in. Every time she opened her mouth, she either started to laugh or cry, and she knew Lillian would have something to say if she spoiled her makeup today of all days. Best not risk her older sister's wrath. So she sat and soaked in the joy surrounding her, enraptured by the glorious snow-covered landscape.

The church was decked out in green and gold, and poinsettias were tastefully placed before the altar. When she and Carter had gathered together with her family and the bridal party yesterday, decorating the social hall for the reception and the church for the wedding had turned into more of a party than a chore.

The limo parked in front of the church. She glanced up at the stone edifice where her family had worshipped the entirety of her life. Gratitude overwhelmed her. Even after she'd left God behind, blaming Him for all her problems and heartaches, He'd still come after her, gently, persevering until she had returned to His flock.

How had she ever doubted the love of her Heavenly Father?

The door to the church opened and her dad exited the church. He'd obviously been waiting for the limo to pull up. He handed her out and guided her into the side door.

During the past year, Vanessa and her parents had grown close again. She'd finally admitted to them all the pain of her past. They'd shed so many tears together, and they'd prayed. Instead of blaming her, her family had moved in closer, surrounding her with their love.

Ten months ago, she'd been shocked when she'd learned the man who'd raped in college had been accused of using a date-rape drug against a colleague. She had gone in and filed her own police report against him. When the woman's lawyer had contacted Vanessa, she'd agreed to help put an end to a serial rapist. With the help of her family, she'd taken the stand and testified. In the end, Nolan had finally gotten what he deserved. It would be decades before he left prison.

And then there was Carter. Carter had been her rock. He'd loved her with a devotion she'd never imagined could be real. When she'd been scared, he'd comforted her and held her. No matter what she said, he never judged her. She couldn't have gotten through it without him.

When the jury came back after ten hours with a guilty verdict, he'd taken her out for a celebration dinner. She'd never forget that night. It was a warm June evening that smelled of sunshine. They'd gone to her favorite restaurant and then out for ice cream at a small ice-cream hut.

She'd felt weightless when they walked along the beach at Presque Isle. And then, Carter turned to her, got down on one knee and proposed.

"I've had this is my pocket since March," he confessed, sliding a velvet-covered box from his pocket. He popped it open, and a lovely gold band with a stunning solitaire ring winked at her. "Vanessa, I love you with all my heart. Will you marry me?"

She attempted to speak over the emotion swelling in her heart but had to swallow and try again. "Yes! Yes, I'll marry you. Today. Tomorrow. Whenever."

He stood and kissed her. She laughed, dizzy with joy.

Then he'd backed up. "Can we— Would you mind if we went and told my mother?"

Carter had introduced her to his mother. Sometimes she was sad. Other times, she was sweet and motherly. Twice, she'd thought Vanessa was her daughter, Gretta, and had cried on her shoulder. Each visit brought pain to Carter. But the care he showed for his mother had proven how great his heart was.

She'd agreed and they'd gone to visit his mother. It was a good choice. Nancy had been in a mellow mood.

"Oh, let me see the ring?" she exclaimed, eagerly stretching out her hand for Vanessa's. Then she'd sighed over the lovely diamond. "Carter, it's just like the one your dad got for me."

Carter had later admitted his mom hadn't talked about his father, who'd died when he was in fifth grade, since the day of his funeral.

Looking around at her bridesmaids and her father now, Vanessa sighed. Carter's mother hadn't lived to see this day. She'd died peacefully in her sleep three months ago. It was sad, but Vanessa had supported Carter through his grief.

"I think God gave us enough time to heal our relationship," he'd confessed to her.

David Hall squeezed her shoulder. She shook off her reverie and looked up at her dad.

"Vanessa, it's time." Her father held out his arm to her. "Are you ready for this?"

She took the proffered arm. "Yes, Dad. I've been ready. Let's go get me married."

The organ began playing Pachelbel's Canon in D. Carter straightened and faced the back of the church. All his nerves fled. This was what he'd waited for. Tanner led Sharon Hall to her pew. Then he rejoined the other groomsmen.

Four lovely bridesmaids floated up the aisle to the groomsmen. Then Brett stepped forward to meet Lillian.

The congregation laughed when the little flower girl danced toward the front throwing rose petals with abandon, followed by Lillian's four-year-old son in his tiny tuxedo.

And then, the organ struck the low chord of the bridal march.

Carter's breath caught in his throat. Vanessa was a vision in white as she moved toward him, her gaze never leaving his. It wasn't until he wobbled on his feet that he realized he was holding his breath. Brett nudged him.

He walked the last few feet to stand in front of the reverend and meet his future. Vanessa's dad kissed her cheek than placed her hand in Carter's.

"Take care of my baby girl."

"Every day of my life," he promised, meaning it with his whole soul.

The rest of the ceremony passed by in a blur. Before he knew it, he and Vanessa were walking down the aisle as husband and wife.

His wife. He couldn't stop saying it to himself. He was no longer on his own. In the past year, he'd lost his mother, the last member of his family. But he'd gained a new family.

He hoped any children they had would have red hair like Vanessa's.

He grinned down at her, amused that he was already thinking of the kids that may come later.

"What?" She smiled at him, a question in her eyes.

"I'm just happy. You're my wife."

"Yep. Which means you're stuck with me now. For good."

He chuckled. "I can deal with that."

The reception flew by. Toasts from Brett and Lillian. Their first dance as a couple. Cutting the cake and greeting all the guests who'd come to share the day with them, even though Christmas was only a week away and they had so many other things to do. He'd never realized just how many friends he had until today.

His favorite part of the day, however, occurred near the end of the reception. Brett and Tanner had led him to a chair in the center of the dance floor. Confused, he'd sat down, knowing this wasn't a normal part of the reception.

The DJ began playing a familiar love song. It took him a moment to recall the tune. It finally struck him that it was about a spouse's promise to always be there for the other, no matter what happened or how time changed them.

Then Vanessa stepped onto the dance floor and began to sing, just for him. The rest of the guests disappeared. He was captivated by her throbbing alto, and all the love in her gaze.

Tears stung his eyes, blurred his vision. He blinked, not wanting to miss a second.

When the song ended, he stood and wrapped her in his arms, holding her tight. "I love you, Vanessa Flint. With everything in me."

She tilted her head back. "I love you, too, Carter. Forever."

Pulling her closer, he kissed her. Around them, their family and friends laughed and cheered. Cameras flashed.

He didn't care. The only thing that mattered to him was in his arms, kissing him back.

He couldn't wait to spend a lifetime showing her how much he adored her.

* * * * *

*If you enjoyed this book,
more titles by Dana R. Lynn
are available now from Love Inspired!*

*Find more great reads at
www.LoveInspired.com.*

Dear Reader,

Thank you for reading Amish Midwife Witness. I hope you enjoyed Vanessa and Carter's story.

I introduced the Hall family during *Protecting the Amish Child*. We didn't meet Vanessa in that book. All we knew was she was Tanner's baby sister. As I thought about her, I realized she had suffered such a huge betrayal, she built an emotional barrier between herself, her family—and God. She needed someone with a strong faith and integrity to help her find her faith again and to learn how to love.

Carter is a new character with his own traumatic past. He tries to be impersonal, but Vanessa's sassy personality is hard to resist. Through her, he discovers it's okay to be emotionally vulnerable.

I love hearing from readers. You can contact me at www.danarlynn.com, where you can sign up for my newsletter to receive exclusive subscriber news.

Blessings,
Dana R. Lynn

Get up to 4 Free Books!

We'll send you 2 free books from each series you try PLUS a free Mystery Gift.

FREE Value Over **$25**

Both the **Love Inspired®** and **Love Inspired® Suspense** series feature compelling novels filled with inspirational romance, faith, forgiveness and hope.

YES! Please send me 2 FREE novels from the Love Inspired or Love Inspired Suspense series and my FREE gift (gift is worth about $10 retail). After receiving them, if I don't wish to receive any more books, I can return the shipping statement marked "cancel." If I don't cancel, I will receive 6 brand-new Love Inspired Larger-Print books or Love Inspired Suspense Larger-Print books every month and be billed just $7.19 each in the U.S. or $7.99 each in Canada. That is a savings of 20% off the cover price. It's quite a bargain! Shipping and handling is just 50¢ per book in the U.S. and $1.25 per book in Canada.* I understand that accepting the 2 free books and gift places me under no obligation to buy anything. I can always return a shipment and cancel at any time by calling the number below. The free books and gift are mine to keep no matter what I decide.

Choose one: ☐ **Love Inspired Larger-Print** (122/322 BPA G36Y)   ☐ **Love Inspired Suspense Larger-Print** (107/307 BPA G36Y)   ☐ **Or Try Both!** (122/322 & 107/307 BPA G36Z)

Name (please print)

Address   Apt. #

City   State/Province   Zip/Postal Code

Email: Please check this box ☐ if you would like to receive newsletters and promotional emails from Harlequin Enterprises ULC and its affiliates. You can unsubscribe anytime.

Mail to the Harlequin Reader Service:
IN U.S.A.: P.O. Box 1341, Buffalo, NY 14240-8531
IN CANADA: P.O. Box 603, Fort Erie, Ontario L2A 5X3

Want to explore our other series or interested in ebooks? **Visit www.ReaderService.com or call 1-800-873-8635.**

---

*Terms and prices subject to change without notice. Prices do not include sales taxes, which will be charged (if applicable) based on your state or country of residence. Canadian residents will be charged applicable taxes. Offer not valid in Quebec. This offer is limited to one order per household. Books received may not be as shown. Not valid for current subscribers to the Love Inspired or Love Inspired Suspense series. All orders subject to approval. Credit or debit balances in a customer's account(s) may be offset by any other outstanding balance owed by or to the customer. Please allow 4 to 6 weeks for delivery. Offer available while quantities last.

Your Privacy—Your information is being collected by Harlequin Enterprises ULC, operating as Harlequin Reader Service. For a complete summary of the information we collect, how we use this information and to whom it is disclosed, please visit our privacy notice located at https://corporate.harlequin.com/privacy-notice. Notice to California Residents – Under California law, you have specific rights to control and access your data. For more information on these rights and how to exercise them, visit https://corporate.harlequin.com/california-privacy. For additional information for residents of other U.S. states that provide their residents with certain rights with respect to personal data, visit https://corporate.harlequin.com/other-state-residents-privacy-rights/.

LIRLIS25